IN THE TIME OF LEAVING

SHANA RITTER

Thank you to family and friends for support, encouragement, belief and helping me find the long quiet spaces. And thank you to readers and listeners for their contributions all along the way.

I am grateful to Bloomington's Women Writing for a Change for their welcoming retreats.

I am also very appreciative of the Indiana Arts Council for awarding me the Indiana Individual Artists Grant, allowing me the time to complete this novel.

PROLOGUE

My name is Chava.

My story is one of leaving. A litany of what I hold in my empty hands; the scent of bread and the sound of horses in the narrow street, the fog rising from the river, the call of the muezzin, the resonant bells of the cathedral. And too, the silence of the synagogue outside its walls, while inside there is the shuffle of men davening, the whisper of women's song descending from the balcony. A mumble of prayer.

These are the things I remember; the shadow of candles on Friday nights and the shape of my mother's hands as she draws them over her eyes, bends her head and welcomes the Sabbath bride. These are the things I thought would become memory but never will; the mikvah I will never submerge in, the chupah in the courtyard, my children playing in the garden under my parents' loving eyes. Instead, I sewed home into the hem of my dress; into the fold of my cloak; into the sleeve of my bodice. I carried with me what I could never return to.

My name is Chava bet Esther. My father was Benjamin, my sister is Sarah. I was born in Toledo, Spain, in the year of 1475. I grew up on the stories of leavings; the crossings of languages; the touch of paper; the smell of ink. My father's family was from the south, Sevilla. My mother's family from the north, Montpellier, in France. All were translators and teachers. Our house was full of words. My father and his friend, Abu Mohammed, often told the stories of their journeys together. They mixed Arabic, Hebrew and Castilian. They quoted Latin verses. They reminisced about a past golden age when Alfonso the Wise was King, and Muslim, Christian and Jew worked together. Stories poured out in a cascade of languages.

We grew up on tales of exile. There was Passover of course, when every year we retold the story of Moses and Miriam leading our people out of Egypt and bondage. Wandering through the desert until they found their home. And then there was the wandering that brought our own families here to Sepharad in the far reaches of the Roman empire nearly a thousand years ago. There were the stories of uprisings in Sevilla in 1391, when so many died or fled, or were forced to convert. They became the Anusim in order to save their children's lives. But this year after the Passover, we will be the ones leaving.

We believed Toledo would be home to us forever, but even before I was born there were rumors that there could be another inquisition. Most believed it would never happen, that it was a threat to extort more money, or gain time to pay back debts. There were a number of our community with close ties to the king and queen, many more who had helped finance the war to reunify Spain. It was Jews who helped Fernando and Isabel wed in the first place, uniting their kingdoms of Castilla and Aragon. How could they want us gone?

There were always rumors. But it wasn't until Torquemada rose in power, appointed to grand inquisitor by the pope himself, that we felt the threat as something real. At first it wasn't directed at us, those who lived outwardly, unapologetically as Jews. The Inquisition was aimed at the New Christians, those who had converted in the last hundred years. It was meant to separate the true believers from the Judaizers, those who secretly continued to be Jews. There were many. Father said Torquemada was like Haman from the story of Purim. He was a man who wanted to be sure that no one remained in his sacred country except those he could control.

We are tied to each other by our stories and our deeds. Our community is a raft, all of us bound together by the cords of our beliefs. Our history is like waves, like currents, like tides. Even when forced by the undertows of necessity, along the ropes of time, we have moved from place to place guided by the pull of the moon; our way lit by our shared words.

Chapter One
Granada Fallen

January 1492

Toledo

Chava went to the window, watching the fog rise from the Tagus. In a few more weeks the storks would begin their return. The nests were still visible in the high steeples of the cathedral. She wondered if when they flew north from Africa over Granada, they would notice the despair left by the war as their shadows crossed the pools of the Alhambra.

Eight years ago, when she was still a child, she had gone there with her family. This rising fog reminded her of the spray of water from the fountains. But in Granada it had been warm and light, not like winter in Toledo. Her father was meeting the caliph about trading and visiting family, old friends and other scholars. She and her sister sat by the pools eating sweets. The women had been so kind, giving them almonds coated with sugar, and water flavored with orange flowers. The sound of the fountains filled the spaces between songs and stories, as the older girls fussed with her and Sarah's hair, making complicated braids and complimenting them on their halting Arabic. Behind them the mountains of the Sierra reached right into heaven; the highest peaks glistening like the bracelets on the women.

The fountains' songs were drowned with the sounds of liturgy. There was no longer any of the sweet music around the inner courtyards and reflecting pools. The Royal family had installed themselves in the Alhambra, their prayers to the virgin and the son and the righteous ways of their faith were somber. They covered the beautiful open scroll work with dark curtains.

People had grown used to the wars. Almost every family had lost a son, nephew, cousin or brother. They accepted their losses because they loved their King and Queen, and the countryside was safer. Fernando and Isabel instilled laws along with conquest. Ever since their marriage in 1469 unified Aragon and Castilla, the King and Queen doggedly led troops to push the Moors out and regain what they saw as the one true Spain. As they drove their armies through the countryside, brigands and robbers no longer thrived. The church answered more directly to the royals. Before Fernando and Isabel there had been disorder. But in the years since their shared rule, while there had been ongoing war, there was also a sense of safety, a kind of peace; unless you were the ones being driven out. Her father was trying to assure that his friends and Granada would be treated fairly, while he remained loyal to the King and Queen, a balancing act he performed dutifully and hoped with some grace.

Benjamin left early most mornings to meet with those closest to the king. He and Abravanel were among those included in the discussions on how to move forward now that Spain was no longer at war. Since his return to Toledo he had felt the cold even more than usual. While the royals celebrated the victory in Granada, Benjamin quietly mourned the loss of the last caliphate in Andalucía. Boabdil had been a good friend, and the Jewish community in Granada had been protected under the Moorish rule. So many rumors floated through the court. Who would rise to power and who would lose? One would think that the end of the war would bring certainty, but instead it raised more questions. No one knew what the future would hold.

CHAVA

The first time I met Queen Isabel and King Fernando, I was five. I was taken to see the new princess in the palace. It was good I had practiced my curtsy because I was mesmerized by the gold on the cradle, the jewels worn by the queen, and the rustle of so many skirts.

I was used to it all by now, father being so often at court. When I asked him why the king and queen called on him so much, he said it was because he offered advice in enough languages that he could both be understood and ignored. From the time I was little, he went away on missions for the king, or was asked to come and consult with the Cortes. This past fall he came back talking about Colon, the Genovese sailor who had once more approached the King and Queen about funds for an expedition. Father was aglow with the thought of it.

"Can you imagine daughters," he told us that night at table, "sailing into seas that you are unsure of, using the maps from the Baleares school and the astrolabe to steer a course? We know the world is round, that it circles the sun the way the moon circles us. Yet there are many who still believe the man will sail to his peril and drop off the earth. The King and Queen understand well the possibilities of finding a new trade route. They understand anything that advances them and Spain. But I am curious to see a different set to the stars. Certainly, the sky must look different from the other side of the great sea.

Sarah looked up then and said, "I bet G-d's voice is different there."

'What do you mean child?" Father turned to her with curiosity, no longer thinking about his stars.

"Away from battle, away from sieges and grabs at power, perhaps across the sea it is simply quieter. Perhaps one can hear the old psalms in the wind."

"What a lovely thought, Sarah,". Father cupped her chin in his hand and quoted from a poem by Halevi, "The star of the east hath come to the west/ He hath found the sun among the daughters thereof"

I thought I could see a place that would echo the beauty of the south, the sounds of the fountains at the Alhambra, full of flowers and small birds. A bit like the poems I learned when we visited the Caliph's family in Granada; the songs were so full of sweetness and color.

In contrast these last weeks of January were weighted with fog. Not the kind of mist that blows away, but a heavy gray laden with crystals of ice. People wore extra layers and when they went out, they would wrap a band of fabric around their mouths and noses to keep the cold out as best they could.

Suppositions on what would happen now that Spain was reunited were flying through every community. Father was worried that Torquemada would try to influence the royals that the Jews must be ousted next. Father had known Fernando since they both were young and had the king's ear. He translated for him often; Fernando trusted him. But Torquemada's influence over Queen Isabel had grown even greater. Within weeks after the conquest Papa found out how quickly the tides were turning in a whispered conversation with the king. He began then to count the gold coins he had saved over the years. He made inquiries and advised my mother about what to do if the rumors came to be. Only some of this was shared with Sarah and me, but enough to make us uneasy.

On the last Friday of the month as we sat at table, after mother lit the candles and said the blessings over the wine and the challah, Father said, "Let us hold hands for a moment. Let us remember how tonight we are warm, and we are together."

We paused and Sarah asked, "Can you smell tomorrow's stew? Chava and I made it, Papa. We sealed the pot with dough and placed it to the side of the fire."

Mama laughed and said, "Maria supervised every step, but the girls did it themselves."

"It will be a feast for us tomorrow.

Chapter Two
Loss and Grief

February 1492

Toledo

Chava came down from the window seat to join Sarah and Esther in the library. They were drawn in close to the fire on this cold morning. Sarah sewed, Esther worked on household accounts, and Chava read a text in Latin that her father had left for her to translate into Castilian. In a few hours, the family would gather for dinner. A lamb stew, simmering in the kitchen, filled the house with the warmth of clove and coriander. They all jumped when the heavy knocker repeatedly hit the front door. Maria opened it and ushered the unexpected visitor to them. "Why Samuel, what a surprise!" Esther began to greet the nephew of Abravenel. But as the young man blanched, Esther stood and asked, "What is it son?"

He leaned toward my mother and whispered, "You must come at once, it is Benjamin."

"What has happened?" Chava asked, as her mother turned to Maria to ask for her cloak.

"Your father is not well, he has collapsed. He is not well…" Samuel's voice trailed off.

"We will come too." Sarah said, her mother already at the door.

"I will go ahead; dress warmly and come. Have Juan come with you."

But just as Esther was leaving, a cart came to their door. Abravenel was sitting next to the driver. Two men were in the back; one was upright and holding her husband's head in his lap. His head shook upon seeing

Esther. "It is too late" Abravenel said. "I am so sorry Esther, he is gone. It happened so fast."

They carried Benjamin into the house and laid him on the table in the dining room. Chava felt her face wet with tears. She had not even realized she was crying. Sarah held her hand, with the other hand she reached for her Papa's still fingers.

"Are you sure?" Esther asked. She recognized the court physician, though at the moment she could recall no other names past her husband's and her daughters'.

"It was as if everything in him stopped cold" the doctor answered. "He did not seem to suffer any pain; he was speaking, then his eyes rolled back, and he fell to the floor. His hand went to his heart, but he didn't speak again."

"What was he speaking of?" Esther asked. The physician looked surprised.

Abravenel took her hand and spoke. "He was talking of setting in place a way to assure the disputation for those of Granada, that it would be fair."

Esther looked at him directly. "Just weeks ago, when he returned from the palace, he said to me here is what you must do if anything happens to me. He made me take down a list of things. Did he know?"

"Perhaps." Abravenel's voice cracked.

Chava took a deep breath. "I will send Maria to Isaac's house to tell them. We will need help to ready him."

Abravenel said, "I will go to the synagogue for the rabbi. I will be back shortly."

Sarah had not said a word. Esther reached for her and Chava and drew them into a hug. She whispered to them so that others could not hear, "Be brave my girls; we will have time to cry soon enough." Then Esther stepped back and ripped her sleeve and the girls did the same. They rented their clothing, tearing it just as their father had been torn from them. It seemed only minutes passed before the room filled. Consolers from the synagogue's burial society came to help the family wash and wrap the body.

Hammering came from the courtyard where a simple coffin was being made. According to tradition, Benjamin would be buried the next morning. As it grew late a few women from the synagogue urged the family to sleep, promising them they would sit with the body. But none of them would leave. Sarah wept softly, Chava recited poems and lines she remembered that her father loved, while Esther remained silent and staunch. It was her way to harden herself when she was most in pain. Later she would cry, there was a whole month of mourning in front of them. Now, they would recite the prayers and give Benjamin the silence and strength he needed to depart.

By the next afternoon, Benjamin was buried. The ground had been difficult to dig, so the men took turns at readying the gravesite. Many came for the funeral. They placed stone upon small stone at the head of the grave. Benjamin had been well loved and respected. The rabbi said of him, "He was a man who understood the weight and beauty of words, as well as being a man who knew how to keep his word."

A year from now his headstone would be placed at his grave and they would gather for the unveiling. They went home for the Shiva. Friends had already covered anything that reflected light, hanging sheets from mirrors and drawing the curtains closed. Plain wooden benches were brought in for visitors. Platters of food and pitchers of drink filled the tables. As was custom, the synagogue's burial society took charge so the family wouldn't have to attend to anything but mourning. For the week of Shiva, the family would do nothing but grieve, sit and pray, eat, tell stories and let their hearts begin to heal. The men would gather to say Kaddish. Privately, in the upstairs bedroom, his daughters and wife would say the prayer of mourning as well.

ESTHER

I am no stranger to death. Benjamin and I had spoken of it many times; not with a sense of foreboding, but simply as one more of the many questions we pondered together. In the same way we argued Midrash over the Torah, talking about death let us examine what we believed about life. Benjamin always had the sense that he would die unexpectedly. He never imagined himself as an old man. So, when his death came suddenly and too soon, I was shocked, yet in a way not surprised. Still nothing prepared me for his absence. Alone in our bedroom I hear his steps across the wide floor planks. His breath is as constant as the sea. I feel as if I cannot stand without falling, but there is nothing to lean on, no one to lean towards. And my poor girls, they will be thrust all too quickly into the womanhood they are already fast approaching. I will not be able to do this alone.

I hear Maria welcome the guests in a soft voice. The men come to form a minion and say Kaddish. Like a small flock of birds, they gather every morning. I try not to think of them as crows. Isaac's voice and his father's, and Abravenel and his nephew, bring comfort; the familiarity of their intonations so like Benjamin's. By custom my daughters and I cannot join them, but we will say Kaddish upstairs in the privacy of our rooms, behind closed doors. Few of the men know that we are doing this, fewer still would approve. In my family the women have always been taught, have always been eager to learn. Below, the men can have their prayers; here above, we whisper and fill our home with our own voices. Our prayer lifts into the folds of the great unknowable.

We come downstairs to sit Shiva. We take our places on the wooden benches in the bare room. The sideboard is weighted with foods brought by friends and neighbors. Usually at a Shiva, voices rise with tales about the one who has passed. But not today, today is silent. We are quiet pondering death which comes too swiftly and too soon. All of us wondering in our own way what we will do without Benjamin.

Those of us gathered are well aware of the changes that are coming. What we do not know is how we will face them, only that it is us left here. But face them we must. People come and go all day and the quiet in the house continues. Though we go to bed early, I don't think any of us will sleep.

On the second morning when the minion gathers, we come down before it's over. We take our seats on the plain wooden benches set in place of the brocade chairs and sofas that usually fill the room. The mirrors are draped in muslin and the windows covered. It seems we are inside a cave thinly dusted with moonlight. Just like our hearts, just like our souls.

After the prayers others begin to arrive, the silence disperses as voices rise telling the stories of Benjamin's life. The house fills with talk and tales, a clatter of plates. By evening I have laughed a few times and watch Chava and Sarah go from laughter to tears and back again as Isaac's father tells about their days as wandering scholars. The trips to Florence to meet with the master book makers there. And the times they went south to the community in Fez. I notice how Isaac stays near Sarah, bringing her food, making sure she has enough to drink.

And so, the first days of sitting Shiva pass, the rough open wounds of our loss beginning to knit closed. The bruising now on the inside, under the skin where it is not so easily seen. There is no getting over death, but one learns to live with loss, to sit next to it; to take from it what it offers, anchoring us here to this earth and to each other.

My husband had been close to the king. He served him for over twenty years. But even so, he understood all too well that he could never give the king all his trust. Even though the king could count on Benjamin, my husband knew how politics could muddle the most righteous of men. On the fourth night the king came simply dressed and with only one bodyguard. He kissed my cheek and called me by my given name. Chava brought him a chair. The space around us cleared. He spoke to me plainly then. He warned me of what I already knew. Before he left, he gave me a finely carved box and said it had been my husband's. He asked me not to open it until a day had passed. I asked Sarah to come and take it upstairs for me. The king nodded.

February 10, 1492

Toledo

By the fifth day, Chava was restless to her bones. Her skin felt dry, her eyes had begun to flit, and she tensed in her seat like a cat who had not quite given up on getting out the door. She sat on one side of her mother, Sarah on the other. She sat and sat. Whether nibbling on roasted garbanzos or bread dipped in olive oil, she had no taste for food. Her father's absence was a hand missing from her shoulder. She kept waiting for his voice asking her to get down a book, to translate a passage; a step on the floor, a punctuating knock on the table. But her father was gone and, in the moments, where she was able to grasp that he would always be gone, it wrenched her heart.

There was no one who would ever understand her in the same way; no one whose eyes would shine with such pride when she quoted a passage from Talmud or knew just the word to translate the notion of morning light from the Arabic. Her father's love pushed her to know more, to do better, to be brave. Without him she was afraid that she would feel weak and listless, her mind catching at phrases she couldn't reach.

More than once her mother took her hand and whispered "This is grief my daughter. It will pass, you will always miss him, but it won't hurt like this forever. He will come to reside with us, his memory will be a blessing."

She would dutifully squeeze her mother's hand, but she wanted to shout at her, at everyone who kept visiting and bringing food and sharing memories and offering condolences, to stop. She would never be whole again. She would always bear the renting of her clothes in the muscles of her heart. She found she could sit still no longer; her foot was jiggling and her hand constantly brushing back a wayward strand. Her mother looked at her, turning Chava's face toward her own she said, "what would help daughter?"

Chava answered nothing, sounding as if she were a small pouting child and not a young woman.

"Think for a moment, close your eyes and tell me what you see," her mother said.

"The fields sweeping by as I ride, the feel of my horse under me, something to carry me, if just for a moment, away."

12

"Go then." Esther said.

Chava's eyes opened wide, "But Mama I can't leave. You know it is forbidden to leave the house."

"You are not leaving. You are only taking a little time to find your breath. Go, go discreetly, but go."

Esther looked to Sarah and asked quietly if she too would like to be outside for a bit. It was a cold day but clear. Sarah shook her head no. "I will stay here Mama. I am best staying here."

Chava gave her mother a kiss on her cheek. In that moment something lifted, a realization that she was not alone. Her mother knew her. She had thought it was only her father who truly knew her heart, but here was her mother telling her to go out and ride. Hearing her before she heard herself. She rose quietly as if she were only going to the kitchen but went toward the back where she found Juan and asked him to saddle her horse. He looked at her quizzically.

"Please" she said," bring her to the back as surreptitiously as you can." She went upstairs and changed into her riding clothes, throwing her cloak over her she went back down through the kitchen and out the back door. Juan was waiting with her horse, Leila, saddled and ready. Out of habit she checked the cinching and took the bridle. Leila was a gift from her father the year she turned thirteen. A beautiful mare that Chava loved at once.

She had been riding since she could remember, but having her own horse was different. She and Leila were intricately connected. Chava always rode astride and had learned to guide the horse with a touch of her thighs, a whisper into her ear as she leaned over her neck. The horse was compact and strong and could glide seamlessly into a fast pace if the way allowed.

She was sure footed in the hills. The mare had her own stubborn streak, but she also loved unabashedly, making Chava and Leila a well matched pair. They trusted each other.

"You are going alone?" Juan asked.

"Yes, I will be back soon." She went through the gate down toward the river and past the bridge to the open fields. There Leila broke into a trot and then a canter. Feeling herself glide through air while Leila held her, she let herself weep. She threw her head back to catch every bit of pale winter sun and was thankful for the wide expanse of sky and the solitary fields. She took the low jump at the stone wall that divided the land and felt herself lifted. She was weightless and yet buoyed by the musculature of the horse and her own strong legs gripping the rippling reach of the flight over the wall.

In that moment, she felt herself soaring free from the gravity of grief. She slowed the horse and draped herself across her beautiful neck. Wrapping her fingers in Leila's mane, she let the mare's strength and patience seep into her. They returned at an easy walk, meandering across furrows over the hard ground, back to the river and the walls of the city. Toledo rose like a mountain into the clear blue of the sky. She heard the cathedral bells shimmer in the naked air. She had heard the bells sounding all her life, marking the hours and the days.

A neighbor saw her approaching and looked surprised but only nodded. She barely nodded back keeping her eyes down, but for a moment a smile lifted her eyes. In that ride she had felt not joy exactly, she was still too sad for that. But the possibility of joy was hers again and for now, that was enough.

Chava gave the reins to Juan when she reached the house and he took the horse. She thanked him and he said, "Anything I can do for you or your family señorita?" She slipped back inside, ran the stairs to her room where she changed clothes. She was soon seated beside her mother. More visitors arrived in the hour before la comida carrying stews, a roast chicken with chestnuts, roasted eggs. It seemed people thought that by bringing what sustains life they could soften grief.

The ride had woken Chava after days of feeling wrapped and muffled. But what heartened her most was that her mother had known what she had needed, even before she did. She saw Esther more clearly than ever before. Her mother had always been there. Though her father was a bright light that had eclipsed her. She would always miss him, but Chava was grateful that her mother was there.

ESTHER

The seven days and nights of sitting Shiva came to a close, but the grief was not gone at all. Maria began to put away the extra plates and dishes and uncover the mirrors. Juan and Jose removed the plain wooden seats from the salon. I was not ready to be a widow, and yet what choice was there. The box the King gave me held a small key and a tiny scroll of paper which had on it only a drawing. I knew what it was, a rendering of the room downstairs, with one small section of the wall shaded. Benjamin has hidden something there for me, but I was not ready to look for it yet. I knew it would be money and jewels. I knew he had worked to secure our safe keeping if ever he should not be able to do so himself.

I imagined the years to come unfolding, the girls marrying. Perhaps in time I will leave and go where it is warm. I could follow others of my family who had long ago gone to the far south near Fez, away from the cold rains and gray days that seem to go on and on here. Maybe Sarah and Chava will join me and I will live near grandchildren in a land where there are always flowers. I have always loved bougainvillea that bloom in the southern reaches and the scent of the warmer sea instead of the fog rising off the cold river and the endless stretch of clouded sky.

Maria asked me what she could do once they finished putting all back to order. I realized more than anything I longed for a bath. With Juan's help she brought the tub up to my room and lined it with muslin and dried flowers. I wanted to soak away the sadness in the hottest water possible. Sarah and Chava had gone for a walk. Lying in the water with steam clouding the room, I could hear Benjamin's voice and feel the warmth that seemed to always emanate from him when he stood close by. It would have to be enough for now. That was all there was.

CHAVA

It was like emerging from a dream. I could remember bits and pieces from the week, snatches of conversation, being coaxed to eat. I can even recall laughter. There were so many stories. Stories about my father's travels; a negotiation gone wrong; a translation by someone that misnamed an instrument that my father rooted out. The only thing I could remember clearly was the ride on Leila, and that my mother had urged me to go. The surprise of my mother suggesting that I leave the house and ride stayed with me. The cold air, bare fields, the merging of earth and sky, this is how I imagine my father now, between memory and spirit.

When I was little and asked, as we all do, "What happens when you die?" I would receive a litany of possibilities. "You become breath. You are

16

born into another life. You lie somewhere between heaven and earth." My favorite answer was that you are like the wind, not seen but felt. Or like the stars during the day, there but not revealed. I had a notion then that you became just a little like G-d when you died.

Our Maria, who had been with our family since she was a girl, believed in her savior with all her heart. She was sure you went to heaven. She described golden gates, the playing of lutes, choirs of angels, and being rejoined with those who had gone before. When I was small, I asked where heaven was, and Maria answered that it was just there above the clouds. For many years I imagined a city in the sky with gated passageways and swirling streets where people gave you nougat and sweet bread and clear cold water.

Once when we were on a walk, I asked my father how a cloud could support the weight of archways and gates and all the people who had died. He looked at me, puzzled for a moment, and then said, "But we spend so many mornings in the clouds ourselves daughter. The fog is a kind of cloud. A cloud is no more than air. The heaven Christians believe in is not perched on clouds. It is a place their hearts have created. Something they can be sure of. They do not much like to live in questions. You know how when we read the Torah, we ponder and ask and argue?"

I nodded my head thinking of the Midrash, the interpretations and discussions, that accompanied the stories of the Torah I had to learn.

"That is not a part of their religion, not for most. They have rules to be obeyed and if they follow the rules, they get the reward of heaven after they die. It's a place of glory where they imagine song and happiness. It frightens me a little."

"You are frightened Papa?" I could not imagine my father scared of anything.

"Well, perhaps frightened is not the right word daughter. We have no heaven or hell, so we must do the best we can everyday of this life here on this earth. We are taught that we must create heaven right here with our neighbors and family. So, when others believe that they can repent for whatever they do and still be rewarded with heaven, it is like permission to do what is wrong. That is what worries me."

"But we all make mistakes Papa. You have told me often that we all miss the mark and must try again."

"Yes, you are right child, that is why we ask forgiveness at Yom Kippur and can try again to do better." I leaned against him and he put his arms around me. "You know my family came from Sevilla. We came because the Christians there wanted us to convert; they wanted everyone to be able to go to their heaven."

"I am confused father."

"It is confusing," he said to me and ruffled my hair. I don't think I was more than six or seven. This was something I would not come to understand until this very Spring when I saw for myself how easily things can turn. How fear lurks beneath the most placid of waters; how when a diversion is taken away, a new diversion must be created. I watched as the victory over the Moors, who were more like us than the Christians in most ways, created the opportunity for them to turn their gaze toward us. When there were no more battles to be won, they decided we were a threat to their Christian sovereignty. We who had lived here for as long as anyone remembered.

I recalled Papa's words, his admonishment to be cautious; to be ready, to know our own hearts and to be sure who could be trusted. Once, after reading the book of Esther he said, "Let's go back and look at the story again. What is it really telling us beyond the brave woman and the loving husband and the evil man who wants power?" He talked about fear, how it can turn into evil and how Haman was a man full of terror who then caused terror in turn.

Only at bed time, when we were quite little, were there stories that were just stories. They would take us to another place or ease a troubling we might be feeling. Most often a story was to tell a truth that was never quite contained in the lines themselves, but rather in the story behind the story. They were stories that would make you want to go back and look at them again in a new way; to ask what would have happened with a different outcome; what can we learn from this and think about that.

I was taught to think that questions were the way to reveal beauty, the way to find the truest melody of something. You questioned and questioned until the outside fell away, until you were left with something shining and real. The words underneath the words, the hum that every good translator learns to hear.

We learned that the Esther of the bible was not a distant someone to be revered. Instead, we were taught that her bravery and loyalty was something to be found in each one of us, especially when things were hard. My mother has always lived into her name. There is always someone like Haman whose fear propels them to want to take away whatever is in front of them and someone else, like Agamemnon, waiting to be shown what can be done. That story of Purim, that we used to act out with costumes and songs, seems all too real now.

We had so many conversations about the holidays, the myths and histories. Why we celebrate each the way that we do. There were few assumptions held in our house.

I was twelve, the first time I fasted for Yom Kippur. It was the thirst I most remember. The way my lips went dry. As much as I tried to lick them wet again, they became drier. The more I tried not to think about it, the more I became aware of it. I thought more of water than remorse; I thought more of water than repentance. I wished the dark would descend and the stars would rise so that I could drink from the botijo, the clay jar where the water had been sitting all day waiting, to take away the parched feeling in my throat, waiting for my lips to fit on the mouth of the jug and drink.

It wasn't the hunger that bothered me. I could wish away hunger but not the want for water. I asked Papa about it after we had broken our fast. He said I had gone into the desert and found the yearning of our people. Yearning cannot be quenched with thought or logic; it can only be satiated with immersion. I must have revealed my confusion in the way I looked at him. He put his hand on my head and promised we would talk more about it in the morning.

That night I dreamt of stars rising in threes, light enough to drown the moon; I dreamt their light turned to water and sparkled in the night. In the morning I went to our library and searched the shelves hoping to find a book or a poem that would explain it to me. Instead I found my father who looked up from the text he was reading and bade me to come sit by him. He stroked my hair back from my face. I had come down in my nightgown without washing my face or combing my hair. He said nothing of this.

"Words will ease you thirst daughter, when there is no water, this is what you should drink." And then he recited a poem to me, I believe it was one he had written.

I have always remembered the last lines, which were as if in answer to my dream. "The light was like a breeze made from wings, as thin as a butterfly's/ for what are prayers but wings that lift us and turn us into light."

Chapter Three

The Alhambra Decree

March 1492

Toledo

In that first month after Benjamin's death the house seemed to be in a perpetual dusk, the dinner table too quiet, the afternoons too long. It was the Hebrew month of Adar, a time when the teachings asked the community to make a strong attempt to bring a note of happiness into their days. In past years there had been lively discussions on the midrash, there had been gatherings and the beginning of preparing for Purim. But not this year, at least not in this house where loss had remained like a glaze of dust on everything and grief seemed a constant hum.

But with the first signs of Spring so too grew the rumors of the coming changes in the court. People stopped by for a quick word with Esther, and soon after began to gather at their home. The house filled with hushed conversations in the library. Sometimes Chava would be called in and asked to translate something from the Arabic or from Hebrew into Castilian or Latin. There were notes about the best routes to take, sending books, families searching out other family members who had left Spain years before.

There was talk of a change in the laws that would be issued within months, others said perhaps weeks that would make Spain a truly Christian land. Prompted by Torquemada the edict would force all of Jewish heritage to make a decision between converting or being forced to leave Spain. As the month went on the conversations became more and more anxious, but whenever Chava or Sarah asked, "Is it sure then, we must leave?" The elders would look at the sisters and assure them, or try to reassure themselves, that the king and queen would come to their senses. They would list the ways the Jews had served the court. The ways in which they were still needed. They would say, "We are physicians, astronomers, their counselors, their bankers." And then the assurances would end with "Still it is always best to be ready." Benjamin was much missed. "His memory is a blessing", they said "but his council is sorely needed."

Chava took up more translating. Sarah took more responsibility for the running of the household and Esther took up more whispered conversations. Chava began to see how much knowledge Esther had, how she was sought out for advice. She carried her opinions and Benjamin's. Benjamin had always shared the news from the court and, most recently, everything the king had intimated. Esther was not prepared for his death, but she was prepared to do what needed to be done.

The Purim holiday came upon them and it no longer seemed like something that had happened long, long ago in distant Persia, where some beautiful queen named Esther, and her uncle Mordechai saved their people from the evil Haman. As children they loved the costumes put on to act out the story, the hard sweet candies received as gifts and most of all the noisemakers they would twirl and shake at every mention of Haman's name. Now they whispered when Torquemada's name was mentioned. The play still went on in the synagogue but the family so soon after Benjamin's death did not have the heart for it.

One evening, the last week of March, Abravenel came to the house. Esther invited him into the library. They stood when he entered to curtsey, but he waved them back into their chairs. Maria brought a tray of hot mulled wine and biscuits. Abravenel paced the length of the room. Chava put down her quill and Sarah stilled her needle. "There is nothing more to be done," he said. "We have tried. If it was just the king, I am sure we could convince him. If there was no Torquemada, we could convince the queen. There is no doubt now that the edict will be issued. It will not be long. I am sorry."

"Tell us what happened."

"Abraham Seneor and I went to meet with Isabel and Fernando; we had a private audience. We offered 30,000 pieces of gold. I saw the king pause, and then Torquemada rushed into the room and said "would you be like Judas?"

Esther gasped, "That madman."

"It was over. Then the Queen looked at Fernando and shook her head. We were dismissed."

"Sit with us for a while. Please. I so miss Benjamin. Your company would be a balm." Esther started to put her hand to her mouth. She did not mean to be so personal, so centered on her own grief at a time when the whole community was in peril. But their old friend put his hand to her shoulder.

"We all miss him. I can't help but wonder if he could have done more. If somehow he could have prevented this from passing." Sarah rose to bring the tray around having told Maria to leave them.

"At least I know that your voice and his would have been the same on this."

Chava took a sip of her wine and placed it beside her "Are you saying, that we will actually be forced to leave?"

"Your father and I spoke of it many times. We discussed different courses of action to take in case the rumor of expulsion became a fact. I have tried my best to carry through all the tactics we discussed, but none of them have worked. Yes, I think it is time to leave. I think you should go now before it becomes official. Before there are more limitations set." He looked from one to the other.

"How can we leave?" Sarah asked, "We are still sorting all of Papa's things, his work. Surely they will grant us time to put things in order."

"It is rumored, that there will be some months from the time the edict is issued until we are made to leave. But do not be fooled. Many will think it will be revoked. Others will believe that it is only a threat. I do not think so."

"How are you so sure?" Chava asked.

"Because child, if they will not be swayed with gold and land at this point, after they have lost so much in the wars, how can we hope anything will persuade them?"

"Perhaps the queen will find her heart in all this. She is a mother, as well as a ruler."

"Ah, ever the optimist, Esther. "

"I will heed your words my friend, but still I have hope."

"Do not hope too much. I fear they will try and prevent us from taking what is ours with us." They spoke then of other times, but when he left, he said again, "Gather what is most important to you. Get ready to be gone."

Esther shook her head and only said, "We will see. At any rate we will have the Passover Seder here before there is any leaving to be done."

CHAVA

Sarah has a way with embroidery. Her tiny stitches render the herbs she loves to tend. Sewing makes me fidget and squirm. Inevitably I prick my finger and stain the fabric. But words, words fly from my fingertips. The direction of the writing shifts left to right and right to left again, like a melody.

Father taught me never to confuse translating a word's meaning with capturing the truth of what was it was saying. Truth was something hidden in between the words, in the implication of a phrase that could be caught most accurately by bending toward the light of the other language. It was not so different from painting, where shades were ways of conveying shadow. Especially when the shadow was something yet to come. "If what we seek is truth," Papa said, "then we must look in the vast emptiness for its echo and listen and be still enough to hear it."

The year before my grandmother died, when I was seven, I asked my father to tell me what it was like before. "Before what?" he asked.

"Before they didn't like us."

"Who daughter, before who didn't like us?"

"The people in Sevilla, where your family used to live." I looked up at him, my eyes level with his middle, waiting. He crouched down then so we could be eye to eye.

"What have you heard, little one?"

"I heard Grandmother talking with Mama saying she was afraid they would start again, like it did in the time when her mother was a child."

"That was a long time ago," he said.

26

"Yes, but so was Passover, and look how that has happened again and again. Mama's family and yours. I am frightened."

I know now that it had been years since any real outbreak had surfaced. Papa was a child the last time a rising swept Toledo and it was against the Conversos, not us. Though I realize now a part of him was always guarded, waiting for a hint, a word from the king. He took my hand and led me to the library. We sat together in his chair. He laughed for a moment, "look how much closer to the floor your feet are then they were just a few months ago. You are growing fast daughter." Then he grew serious again, "People hate what they fear child, and they fear what they do not understand. The church becomes afraid of us because we challenge them to think differently than they have been taught."

"I don't understand lots of things, but it doesn't make me hate them, it makes me want to know more."

"That my child is because you have a special turn of mind."

"But why Papa, why is Grandmother afraid?"

"Remember the stories that my father tells from his father, about what had happened in Sevilla, almost a hundred years ago? They wanted the Jews to convert, to become Catholic. They say they wanted to save their souls, but they did not want others around them who believed differently."

"And we fought them with swords the way the King and Queen fight the Moors?"

"No, we fought them by being obstinate, and being flexible," he said.

" Papa you are not making sense. How can you be both?"

"Well many of us were obstinate, we refused to convert, and we left. We took everything we owned and went to other places and started again. And some of us were flexible- we pretended to convert but we didn't. You know how we have friends who keep a statue of the virgin by their door, but hide a mezuzah in her foot? Some kept faith on the inside and pretended on the outside."

"But isn't that lying?"

"Lying is when you are untrue. The Anusim, those that were forced to choose between their lives, their family's lives, or their faith, pretended because they felt it was the best way to keep everyone safe."

"Then why is Grandmother afraid?"

"Well those that wouldn't leave and those that wouldn't pretend some of them were hurt very badly."

"Who hurt them?"

"The people who most feared them. Christians who believed they could be taken over by Jews or Muslims; perhaps those that didn't believe enough in their own ways, or in themselves."

"Or maybe, Papa, they believed so much they wanted everyone to think like them."

"Well child, let me ask you this, do you believe in who you are?"

"Of course. I am Chava bet Esther and daughter to Benjamin and sister of Sarah and…"

"Do you want other people to be you?"

"How could anyone else be me Papa? You have always said that each person is unique."

"Exactly daughter, and someone else being them does not bother you, being you?"

"No Papa. So why do the Christians want the Jews to not be Jews?"

"Perhaps daughter they don't really believe in their own ways as strongly as they pretend."

Chava shook her head. "I still don't understand then why Grandmother is afraid Papa, should I be too?"

"Be wary, but don't be afraid, Grandmother is full of memories and those memories become stirred. You don't have those thoughts buried in you, but stay wary daughter, be vigilant, but not afraid. Fear makes people do strange things."

"And you Papa are you not full of memories?"

"Not as much as my parents, and not as little as you. I am in the middle daughter, enough to know to stay awake, and too few to not let me sleep. It is getting late now."

"Yes Papa." I leaned into his chest. Here, with him in the library, I could not imagine any place safer. I remember how I grew sleepy against him.

"Come child I will carry you up to bed. I wager your sister is already asleep." As he tucked me beneath the quilts, next to Sarah, I asked him what should I dream of?

"Dream of the stars, child, moving across the heavens; dream with the angels daughter."

Oh, how I wish I could talk to him now.

March 22, 1492

Toledo

It is Esther who rises first and goes to sleep last. She makes sure everything is in order and everything that must be done, is done. She wakes in the middle of the night, in the darkest dark, with a feeling of a hand on her shoulder, a sense of a whisper in the room. She misses her husband. Betrothed since they were young, they had loved each other for many years.

First as a hope, a whisper of possibility. Then later as something to be discovered, a whole new world, a geography to transverse. The difficulties of having children, those first deaths, had given them a vocabulary of loss, a shared grief that tinged their days. Their surviving daughters gave them a shared joy.

The infidelities of the court sobered their view of the world, making them both more cautious and more daring. The court was simultaneously steadfast and mercurial. Constant in its drive to reunite Spain as a Christian land, and ever changing in how that would be done, and who would best serve the campaign at hand. It was like steering a ship through dangerous waters. You had to be alert to wind and current, trust the boards under your feet, but not be too afraid to change course as the sea demanded. All this they had done and had done it together.

Their library, and the wealth of manuscripts it contained, had been passed down from both sides of the family. After the uprising in Toledo, some forty years before, more care was taken about assuring its safety. So many did not know how to read and imagined the pages held some secret to be used against them, the written word became a target. Most people had never heard the poetry of Hafiz or the sayings of Maimonides or seen the patterns of the stars and the patterns of numbers written down upon a page. Most people did not know that knowledge was a commodity they could have, and so it became something to be scorned and done away with, something to be burnt and destroyed.

There were shelves behind the shelves and drawers that appeared to not be there, where pages and scrolls were stored with cedar chips and other spices that would keep insects at bay. The translators felt it was their responsibility to protect that which was contained in the writings and assure that it could be passed down for generations yet to come. They felt it was their most important legacy.

Each of the primary families, from the school of translation, had preserved some of the books in their own homes so that they would be a less visible target than the school itself if fear should once again erupt and destroy as before. What had not been foreseen, though at the same time it was not a great surprise, was the hatred toward the community aroused by the Inquisition and sanctioned by the court. When the royals placed their signatures on the edict of expulsion, they condoned what they had tried to keep at bay for many years, a unified scorn, a holy hatred against all that was not under the roof of the church. Once again, the words were in peril; the body of knowledge that had been kept safe and expanded on would be confiscated, at best hidden away, at worst burnt and lost forever.

ESTHER

I learned to hold a quill when I was only three, though the markings I made with it barely resembled letters. Still, I understood that what was written on a page stayed even if the page was lost. My father was a translator as my family had been for as many generations as we knew. My oldest brother went to the Portuguese court when I was nine. My sister married the year before and my other brother studied in Salamanca. By the time I was five, I could make my letters in Hebrew and Castilian. By the time I was eight, I could write well in Arabic. My grandmother always spoke to us in French, so I knew that as well.

I was the only one still at home and my father needed a helper he could trust, so he taught me the art of translation. I practiced diligently on scraps of vellum and on my wax board. Useless at embroidery or any fine stitching I continued to help my father until I married at 18, and then I helped Benjamin. My girls have the same skill, though truthfully Sarah would rather sew than write, Chava however is either at a desk or on a horse.

Long ago my family had been a part of the great medical school at Montpellier, in France, as doctors and translators. But they were ousted hundreds of years ago when some great fear rose up louder than needs or reason and the community was made to leave. They sailed to Valencia then came here to Toledo. My great, great grandfathers helped to found the school of translators in Toledo and contributed to the building of the synagogue. We are as rooted here as we ever were there. We added our own exodus from Montpellier to the Passover story every year, and the old French songs were sung at the close of Shabbat each week.

What makes a place home? Knowing the stones at the doorway to the house by finger's touch; stepping over the casement without thinking about how high to lift your foot; following the hallway to the library and reaching to the shelf where the book you are thinking of is carefully placed; laying the table for Shabbat dinner and hearing the echo of prayers before they are said. Those are memories that can be carried. The Christians leave flowers by a grave. We leave a stone to mark our visits. We leave something of the earth that will not fade or die; something solid that can be felt; something of substance that can be carried in one closed hand. We leave behind the weight of the stones but take the remembrance of their shape with us.

I always knew who I was, where I came from, but what I had no idea of is that this story of leaving would repeat itself these generations later with my own daughters. Do I dare imagine some great, great grandchild telling the stories of our life here in yet another faraway place?

Chava came to find me as I was in the herb room tending the plants we bring in each fall. I was trimming back parsley. She is taller than I am now, but she leaned and rested her head on my shoulder. We both stood there silently for some time, looking through to the kitchen garden and beyond to the valley and the river. I remembered so clearly Chava as a little girl of four. She was my strong little girl, the first of my children to survive to that age. Two year old Sarah was asleep, and I listened for her sighs. I felt so at peace in that moment, my girls safe and near me. And Chava, leaning against me, brought back that same sense of contentment. I took it in as those moments had been absent since Benjamin's death.

My thoughts had been much more with the grief that filled me when I lost my two sons one after the other, and then the next child lost too soon to know if it was boy or a girl. In the years that followed, before I became pregnant with Chava and soon after Sarah, I thought I might never have a child. And then, as first Chava and then Sarah thrived, that despair was dissipated by my love for them.

The stones of my family's losses have shaped my hands and the bounty of my family's blessings have given me strength. I was taught to believe that it is in this world that you make your choices and receive your gifts as well as your curses. The Christians think they are preparing for some holy and beautiful ever after. Their popes and cardinals and bishops will welcome them to the gates of their heaven and their golden tables. The ones who want us to convert say they are trying to save our immortal souls. What they don't know is that each deed, each day, is its own heaven. My daughters are all the blessings I need.

Chava turned to face me and asked, "Who will plant these when we are gone? It has always been Sarah's job."

"She will do it just before you leave. The weather is turning mild already and you still have a little time."

"I do wish you'd come with us, Mama."

"We will be together again before too much time has passed. I need to see to things here first. We have been over this before, Chava. You need to leave soon. They will not be checking things as thoroughly in these early weeks. It will become more and more difficult to assure the safety of the manuscripts as time goes on."

"But Papa would have wanted us to stay together." She begins the same argument, strengthened by the letter we found in the library.

"It's me who needs to make the decisions as to what is best for all of us now, daughter. You know it saddens me to be apart from you and Sarah, but it is what is best for now. At least this is what I believe, and I need to trust in that."

I see her shoulders tighten and her chin begin to jut out, which always led to her stamping her foot when she was a very young girl. But she controls herself and with a shudder only a parent would recognize, she says "Yes mama." She gives me a kiss on the cheek, but I know my daughter has not given up yet. There will be more discussions in the days to come. She will learn where she really gets her stubbornness from and it is not her father.

The night the gazelle displayed to me/her cheek-the sun-beneath a view of hair…

Imagine this line of Halevi's becoming ash. That is how I began to lay out the plan to assure that we will preserve our legacies, the manuscripts of translations, the books we have guarded so carefully, our shared inheritance. I spoke first to Abravenel and Seneor, then to my girls. I wanted to be sure my daughters fully understood. As each step of what needed to be done became clearer to me, so too did the feeling of Benjamin guiding me become plainer.

Torquemada was the one to really be feared. He had the influence to have the king sign the edict, who knew what else he might bring about? If the Jews and Muslims were banished from Spain how long then until science and math were overshadowed by his teachings? How long until what is right and just will be gone as well?

I know loss all too well. The loss of my children and my husband. The impending loss of my daughters to another land. I will not have generations of work gone, condemned into smoke, in order to soothe the fears of those who do not honor learning. I will not lose our voices. This I can do. Those who cannot read or write, oh I wish they could, have no sense of how words can rise off the page; how they can create scent, light and even the texture of fabric to the fingertips. It might be a story that traces the life of a family until it is a Roman built road you are walking on; walking west and west toward the sun setting and the moon rise. The weight of words turns buoyant. I have slept with words dancing around me; I have seen them rise off the page and become a road that led me where I was supposed to go. I will not have all this turned to ash, even if it costs me what is left of my life.

The plans were to send the manuscripts and documents out a few at a time with each family, more hidden within shipments of goods, others as letters. But it would need to be done quickly, while it was not suspect. We would need to keep records of where everything was sent and in whose keeping. While the royals thought the Jews would be tending to their personal affairs of land and money, we would seize the advantage and save our history. There were enough of us who understood that this was more valuable than the land and goods we would need to relinquish. It gave us the chance to hide our knowledge and our heritage behind the obvious things they thought we would want to save.

Each family that was part of the school of translators had a catalogue of their libraries. Duplicate works would go to different places. There would have to be some decisions made, of course, on what to forfeit and what to save. The same would be true for everything. Was it not always so?

But even as I make the lists, draw out plans, write the necessary letters, work with the others to set the arrangements in motion, I feel pieces of me are scattered like dust on stones. I look at my daughters and remember when I was young. How full of hope I was when I was getting ready to marry. Looking at their future, or what I can imagine of it, hurts terribly because what is happening to them will pull their lives apart. They will lose pieces of themselves in the in between. Flakes of skin, scints of bone, their hair, eyes, and teeth, some parts of who they are will forever remain here in Toledo. And the women they become will be in some foreign place.

It is a mother's despair that shrouds me like the sheets of a corpse. It is not that I will die when they leave. I will live on, but none of us will remain whole. Perhaps that is the case for everyone; we are never who we were before. There are changes that shape us and make us shed ourselves so that we can be shaped again. Still, this is not just shedding but also dismembering, this is pulling us apart from ourselves. I could wail. I could keen. I could scream. Yet, I will do none of those things, none of them.

I wish I could pray the prayers of real asking; the prayers in which you lose yourself in the invocation of words. There are the prayers of gratitude and the prayers of promise, but what is inside me now are the prayers of questions. I am not feeling brave. I am not even wanting to be brave, and yet I hear my husband's voice saying you will be brave. I can feel his hand run from the crown of my head to the side of my cheek. The warmth of it there, a comfort so deep, old and familiar, that I feel callouses on his fingers gently scratch against my face.

Benjamin and I did not have a marriage based on formality, nor one always of agreement, but we did have a true union of partners. There was much love between us, and perhaps even more a respect and a willingness to reach out and to offer up. My daughters always watched us closely and they will not settle for less. That is why I know Sarah will wed herself to Isaac, and why I am saddened by Chava and Daniel's dissolution. I don't know if Chava will find a partner equal to her. This worries me. There are not so many men who will let the strength of their wives shine the way my older daughter is meant to, and she is meant to.

I was blessed to have a father who knew this and made sure my husband was a man who understood it as well. There was a time I thought Chava and Daniel so perfectly matched. I see the way Sarah and Isaac look at each other; anyone can see that. If Benjamin hadn't died, they would be betrothed by now, but she will have to wait for her uncle and aunt to see to it. They know already that we have given our blessing.

Maria thinks I should go with the girls but has given up arguing with me. She will keep my secrets. For now, the plans are laid, and I lay myself with them. I am done with arguing, done with it. I have no stomach for it anymore. Let the scholars sing their songs of discourse. I just want quiet and to know my girls are safe.

March 30, 1492

Toledo

When sleep was not possible, even though she wanted nothing more than that oblivion, Esther made lists in her head of what needed to be done. She sorted and counted books and planned what food to pack for the journey so the children wouldn't have to stop at an inn and eat traif. She would plan what clothes should be taken and what the hems or folds of fabric could hide. Memories of making clothes for the girls when they were small came unbidden; a pleasure in the evenings, as she and Benjamin spoke while she sewed. Esther had been over thirty when Chava was born, but she felt like a young mother. She walked with her all over the city, wanting to share everything with her.

Esther still missed each of the children that she buried. She whispered their names more often than anyone knew. She spent more time with her daughters than any of the women she knew. They had a nurse to help with the children, and once they became older, a tutor. But she and Benjamin took on the primary teaching of both girls in all matters, whether household practicalities, reading and writing, translation, the preparation of foods, the mending of clothes, or the planting of the household gardens.

The raising and care of their daughters took on a liveliness and a sacredness for both of them. Not just a shared sense of responsibility, but possibility. They couldn't help but see in them all of the other children who had left their lives too quickly. There were times both Esther and Benjamin needed to be gone, but she would try and make her stays away from home as brief as possible. She began to take the girls with them at a time when many others were glad to be away from their children.

Esther was relieved that as a Jewish woman she had never been asked to be a lady in waiting to the queen or to be part of the court. She didn't

38

know what she would have done if she had to be separated for long lengths of time from her daughters. Their days were filled with an ease that came from working side by side. She and Benjamin made sure their heads were full of languages and stories, facts and figures. They never knew then how well it would serve them once the leaving came. When Benjamin had been alive, she slept soundly each night, tired from a day filled with chores that needed doing. Even when he was away, she could feel his presence beside her. But these lengthening days brought less sleep and more worries. Was she making the right decision? Would her children be safe? Just this afternoon she had nearly dropped the platter she was carrying.

Maria looked at her and seeing the exhaustion there, she took the dish from her hands and said, "You must sleep mistress." She made her a tea then and brought it to her. Esther slept a long siesta. When she woke, she felt more rested than she had in a long while and also calmer. She would have to ask Maria what was in the draught, or perhaps it was better not to know. That night she slept again. And in the morning when she woke just a little past dawn, she felt capable of all she had yet to do. She sorted through Benjamin's clothes to give to the temple and searched for a memento for his brother and another for Isaac. Each would treasure something of his to keep, she thought. His wedding ring she kept for herself, wearing it on the thumb of her other hand.

Chava loved this time of year with its turning weathers, changing days and returning light. It gave her more time each afternoon to read by the window. She loved the way the hues in the fields made her mother's eyes bluer, instead of winter gray. It seemed like everything grew light as spring came; it brought with it the Passover, the cleaning out, the coming of family and gatherings of friends. That was every year until this one. This one was the one that marked a whole new way of looking at Spring.

There were many paths to the river. One straightforward to the main plaza and then down the hill to the banks of the Tagus. But the path the girls liked best, and had ever since they were children, was the one that meandered through the small streets and alleys and opened out from one of the town gates to the fields. The city walls circle the curve of stone down to the river. It is the way they most often went when sent on an errand that was not urgent, or when they were given the chore of taking a message to one of the boats that had come to the port. Most often, it was a letter sealed with their father's official seal that carried some tally or request to be taken to the next city or village.

The river was the fastest way to carry news, goods and messages between Toledo and Portugal. Across the far-reaching plains of lower Castile, the river made its way until it reached the Atlantic. There were tributaries all along it that smaller boats would use when meeting the larger vessels midway between the banks, so there would be no danger of running aground.

In the cold days of winter, there was little traffic on the water; the fog covering the banks, cloaking everything. In the spring, with little warning, it could shift from clear days to days laden in fog as the ground warmed and the countryside changed from brown to green; the flowering coming between. The wind would carry the sweet scent of almonds and the promise of long afternoons stretching into long evenings.

Storks began the return to their nests in the high towers, flying all the way from Africa across the Mediterranean and resting only briefly on their journeys. That is how at least the people of Toledo thought of it. The storks

40

were returning home. Chava wondered out loud to her father, if the people in Africa thought the same- that when fall turns to winter, the storks return home to them? Her father had answered, with a smile, that he supposed so and that everyone liked to claim beauty and name it as their own.

CHAVA

"Listen hard. Can you hear it?"

"What Papa?" Sarah and I would chant in unison. We knew the answer that was coming, and it made us want to hear it all the more.

"The hundred ways I love you." And he would start chanting phrases in all the languages he knew, and then make up some as well. It wasn't just words, but the songs of the birds, the different sounds of the winds, the movement of water and the ways the trees grew; things I didn't even know had a name.

Once Sarah and I were past our toddling years, father had a beautiful bed made for us. Up and down the posts were birds, butterflies and flowers, and phrases in Arabic and Hebrew, Castilian and French that proclaimed how much we were loved and cherished. The stars were painted on the ceiling above our bed so that as we fell asleep, we were reminded of the wide breath beyond this world.

This past year before Papa died, I hardly traveled with him at all. Father knew that he needed to be indispensable to the king and queen, as did Abravenel, Seneor and the other Jews who advised the court. They felt they could not let their importance be doubted for even a second. They never wanted to remind the royals that as Jews we had more in common with the Moors they were trying to conquer than we did with them. We shared the same Sabbath and ate much of the same foods. We appreciated the science of the stars and the arc of numbers in a way the Church did not. We knew we lived on the periphery no matter how often we found ourselves called into the center. We knew very well who ruled.

Papa was gone more than usual from the spring into the fall. He conferred with the king and queen as they advanced in their taking of Granada, the last Muslim caliphate. It seemed the more they talked about Spain's Christian reunification, the more they asked the Jews for council and money. It was not only the special taxes we paid that financed the war, but the loans we advanced to Isabel and Fernando as well. I heard Papa speak with other translators and scholars bemoaning the fact that they had been born into the wrong time. If only they had lived under Alfonso X, two hundred years before they could have spent all their time in the conquest of knowledge and not as advisors and financiers in the conquest of land.

Toledo had been at the center then; a place where ideas spilled from Arabic into Hebrew, Latin and Castilian. The school of translators worked in teams. Christians, Muslims and Jews translated the stories of Baghdad, medical texts, manuscripts on astronomy, Greek texts, the poems of Rumi and Halevi, the Quran and the Torah. The air was thick with words, like herb gardens filled with colors and scents. It makes me giddy to think about it.

There were stories about debates over theocracy and science. Contests were held not just to see who could win but to illuminate ideas, to expand and expound. People came from Fez and Constantinople, from England and France to study and teach in Toledo. They followed the old Roman roads to my city to talk about the meaning of words and the measurements of the sky and reach of the seas. I often wished I had been alive in that time though there were even fewer women who were permitted access to the books and conversations. I would have found a way though. I am sure of that.

It is done. The edict of expulsion has been drafted. Samuel, Abravenel's nephew, came to the house last night. The proclamation of the Alhambra, as the King and Queen are calling it, has not yet been made public, but shared in the court. Quickly, a few copies were made to be brought to the community. It will be issued as law all too soon, and then we will have but a short time to be gone. Whether we choose to be gone from Spain as Jews, or gone from being Jews to become Christians, we must give up much of what makes us who we are.

I offer Samuel mulled wine, but he says he must go to the next house and then the next. He tells me Abravenel and Seneor are still trying to change their minds, but there is little hope. His last words are "ready yourselves." Then he was gone, and we were left with a copy of the edict which was being called The Alhambra Decree.

Therefore, we, with the counsel and advice of prelates, great noblemen of our kingdoms, and other persons of learning and wisdom of our Council, having taken deliberation about this matter, resolve to order the said Jews and Jewesses of our kingdoms to depart and never to return or come back to them or to any of them. And concerning this we command this our charter to be given, by which we order all Jews and Jewesses of whatever age they may be, who live, reside, and exist in our said kingdoms and lordships, as much those who are natives as those who are not. Who, by whatever manner or whatever cause have come to live and reside therein, that by the end of the month of July next of the present year, they depart from all of these our said realms and lordships, along with their sons and daughters, menservants and maidservants, Jewish familiars, those who are great as well as the lesser folk, of whatever age they may be. They shall not dare to return to those places, nor to reside in them, nor to live in any part of them, neither temporarily on the way to somewhere else nor in any other manner. Under pain that if they do not perform and comply with this command and should be found in our said kingdom and lordships and should in any manner live in them, they incur the penalty of death and the confiscation of all their possessions by our Chamber of Finance, incurring these penalties by the act itself, without further trial, sentence, or declaration. And we command and forbid that any person or persons of the said kingdoms, of whatever estate, condition, or dignity that they may be, shall dare to receive, protect, defend, nor hold publicly or secretly any Jew or Jewess beyond the date of the end of July and from henceforth forever, in their lands, houses, or in other parts of any of our said kingdoms and lordships, under pain of losing all their possessions, vassals, fortified places, and other inheritances, and beyond this of losing whatever financial grants they hold from us by our Chamber of Finance.

And so that the said Jews and Jewesses during the stated period of time until the end of the said month of July may be better able to dispose of themselves, and their possession, and their estates, for the present we take and receive them under our Security, protection, and royal safeguard, and we secure to them and to their possessions that for the duration of the said time until the said last day of the said month of July they may travel and be safe, they may enter, sell, trade, and alienate all their movable and rooted possessions and dispose of them freely and at their will, and that during the said time, no one shall harm them, nor injure them, no wrong shall be done to them against justice, in their persons or in their possessions, under the penalty which falls on and is incurred by those who violate the royal safeguard. And we likewise give license and faculty to those said Jews and Jewesses that they be able to export their goods and estates out of these our said kingdoms and lordships by sea or land as long as they do not export gold or silver or coined money or other things prohibited by the laws of our kingdoms, excepting merchandise and things that are not prohibited.

Chapter Four

Readying to Leave

April 1494

Toledo

CHAVA

If you listen carefully, you can hear the trace of accent in my mother's voice. It's in the melody of a prayer; the recipe for a Sabbath stew. The family stories tell of Montpellier in the south of France, of our home near the synagogue and the mikvah, the arbors of grapes, the sweet-sharp scent of lavender, the proximity to the sea. All these I grew up with as if they had been in my own childhood. How could my mother and grandmother and great grandmother carry those stories as if they were yesterday's doings and not so long ago.

I remembered in my grandmother's home, there was a clay jar that held some small amount of earth from their home in Montpellier. It had been her family's home for many centuries, just as Spain has been the home of my father's family for so many generations had lost count. And yet, it seems we are always looking for home. That is the daily bread of our lives. The sustenance of who we are as a people. We ask the way and we seek to find it.

When the rumors began that we would be forced to leave Toledo, I pictured my grandparents, all gone from us now, shaking their heads saying again, yet again. My mother's family made their way south when the expulsion order was issued and they had to leave Montpellier. There my great-great-grandfather had been a professor in the school of medicine. For part of the journey, they accompanied Christian colleagues along the road of the great pilgrimage to Santiago. It was safer to travel in large groups.

My mother's family, like my father's, had always had relationships with Christians and Moors. Even with the stark differences there was enough common ground. Even if only bread was shared in regard to food there was much to share in terms of conversation. Long ago, between those who dealt daily with each other there was a "deaccuerdo", an agreement known but rarely spoken. This let the differences between their faiths be like silent observers to everything that crossed between them, whether trade of ideas, or trade of goods. Those that knew the languages and ways could move between worlds and bring what one world knew into the other without disturbing too much of the geography of their daily lives.

All those tales of leaving are a part of who we are. The Portuguese have a word, saucede, which means longing for what is now gone, a bittersweet remembrance. Dwelling, just for a moment, in what can no longer be. I hear it in our prayers. Even when there is exaltation, there is sadness. I think it is always missing home; a place where you truly belong. A place you will never be asked to leave.

ESTHER

Last night as we cleared the supper, Sarah turned to me, "Mama it worries me to leave you behind. What if you cannot leave before the last date? What if they question you? What if they force you to convert?"

"So many questions, Sarah. I believe the best way to be a good Jew is to live. First and foremost, we must survive. We are learned; we are landholders. We have responsibilities. I do not say this from pride or greed.

I say this because of purpose. For what is a life without purpose? It would not be mine."

"But Mama," my youngest objected, "you can find purpose coming with us. You can assure that the stories you have always told us were so important will survive."

"Ah hija, you and your sister can do that. I have been a good teacher, have I not?"

And with that Sarah bowed her head. Checkmate I thought; there was no way to win. Chava would have kept on arguing, but Sarah knew when the game, at least this game, was over. She wasn't ready to give up yet; she was just quieter about it than her older sister. She would bide her time. She did not want to leave without me; I knew. It was enough to have lost her father.

When Sarah was a young girl, it was possible to forget that she was in the room. Many times her quietness belied her keen eye. She was a child who watched and noticed, remembered. Chava did enough talking for them both, enough moving, enough yelling, enough insisting. It wasn't that Sarah was malleable, so much as she chose her battles carefully. She was not shy to use subterfuge when it suited her. If something was important enough, she would find a way. It's just that not as many things were as important to her.

There was a large chair Sarah liked to hide behind. She became very good at being so still that she would blend into the shadows of the room. She learned to keep her breath quiet and even become one of the sounds of the house. She would wait for someone to come into the room and then would listen to the conversations and remember. Sometimes she would relay them to Chava; sometimes she would just keep them to herself.

April 5, 1492

Toledo

"Daughters come to the library." Esther sat in the chair that would have been Benjamin's. They had not lit the fires as it had been an unusually warm day. Waiting there for Chava and Sarah, Esther looked at the shelves now half empty. There was still a lot of work to do.

"Yes, Mama." Sarah came and kissed her on the cheek. It was just past the hour of the siesta, but no one had slept. Chava stood in the doorway, her eyes scanning the room, and then looked quickly down. She had to blink back tears. Esther saw her downcast expression.

"I know it is disheartening to see the room growing bare. But think of the books we are saving."

"I try and tell myself that Mama, honestly I do, but all I keep thinking is what we are losing."

"The books were never really ours, Chava. We were just their keepers."

"It's not that we don't have the books here it's that..." Her voice broke.

"What Chava?" Her sister came by her side and took her hand. It was so unusual to see Chava shaken.

"I won't be able to study. Who will keep teaching me? I can hear the disparaging questioning. Why do you want to study? You are just a girl."

"Do you think we all have not faced that? You continue even if it is just you and the words."

"But Mama you had your father and then Papa. You had books, I will have..."

"You, child, will have your own good mind and you are taking some manuscripts and books with you. You will find…"

"How do you know, Mama? How can you know what we will find?"

"Chava, we are not going to the ends of the earth, just to Portugal."

"Sarah, Portugal is just the first place we will go; the world is changing fast. The Portuguese court won't be far behind. Do you not see?"

"Come sit now." The girls sat on the bench in front of Esther. Chava bit her lip and Sarah looked questioningly at them both.

"But mother, you said it would be temporary; you said…" Sarah's doubts rose in a rush.

"I know what I said, Sarah. Chava is thinking of a future she cannot know."

"I have an idea mother. I listened long and hard to the conversations between Abravenel, father and Seneor. You know how often they spoke of this."

Sarah's hand pressed into fists. "Tell me what you're both meaning."

Esther and Chava began at the same time. Esther gave her daughter a sharp look. Chava apologized, "I am sorry mother, I did not mean to interrupt."

"Girls, Chava is right in that we cannot be sure what the future holds and certainly things are changing in the court. But we do not know what the outcome will be. There are still many who think the king and queen will call us back. Portugal will only be temporary. And sending the books away is only an extra precaution."

"Please Mama may I speak my mind?"

"When have you not, Chava?"

"I don't think it will be temporary. Sarah, I don't want to disillusion you. I don't want to hurt you. But I don't think we are coming back."

"Well I do." Sarah looked like she would stamp her foot as she had when she was little. She had her arms crossed in front of her, holding herself.

"You can each believe as you will. I cannot change that; I can only love you both. I don't know if anyone really knows what will happen. We can only…"

And Chava filled in with the phrase they had always heard their father say, "do what we can do to give the world as much light as possible."

"Come and help me with the books on this shelf Chava. They still must be sorted to see what goes where." Chava rose and got the small stool from beside her father's desk. "Sarah, please go and help with the garden. Maria is laying out the herbs for planting." Sarah nearly skipped out of the room but stopped to give her sister a quick peck on the cheek.

"Mother, do you really believe this is only temporary?" Chava asked, once Sarah was away.

"I believe that what will be was meant to be, as long as we do what we can."

"Not a real answer, Mama."

"As best as I can do at the moment, daughter. Hand me that book, the one with the silver Arabic on the spine. The book of poems. I shall keep that."

"Was it a gift, Mama?"

"From your father."

Chava opened the book at random and began to translate, "Come into my garden at the moment the sun lets loose the scent of the orange flowers. Mama!"

"Your father knew his verses, Chava. When we were younger, he often recited some of Solomon's songs to me."

"Oh Mama, you loved each other well, did you not?"

"That we did. I was blessed. We all were. Take that blessing with you when you go."

ESTHER

My father often said things happen in threes. The question is when do I begin to count?

Over a year ago was the breaking of Chava's betrothal to Daniel. They were promised as children, but then his family made the decision to convert. I know it was not taken lightly. I think they knew, even then, that there would be changes coming and they wanted to protect themselves. Unlike us, they had many in their family who had already converted. Louis Santangel was a cousin; perhaps he warned them even before Benjamin was warned. They asked Chava to convert and wed Daniel as planned. But she would not, nor did we want her to.

It broke both their hearts, even as young as they were. How did we know then there would be so much more to break our daughters' hearts? Just as we were beginning to rise up from the blow of Benjamin's death the edict came down. We knew it would come, but still we were not ready. Daniel's family resettled near Barcelona. They felt more protected there, accepted into the larger community of "New Christians".

Or do I begin the counting with Benjamin's death? I only know my days are filled with readying my daughters to leave. How fitting it is that it is the time of the Passover as well. At least we do not have the plagues; at least we do not have to run, not yet. I pack items to give to the poor. I choose the smallest, finest things for Chava and Sarah. I observe the capable women they have become, but I can't help but think of the girls they so recently were, before death and impending exile cast their shadows. We cannot know the sweet without the bitter, nor wholeness until something breaks. It is only then that the tenuousness of our lives is illuminated. There is an old saying that light makes its way through the crevices of shattered things.

I hold a memory of a morning years ago, on a day Benjamin returned from one of his journeys for the king. The girls halted as they came down the stairs; Sarah just a step higher than Chava. They looked from me to the baggage their father had left when he returned just before dawn. They hadn't known he was back. The joy of his homecoming illuminated their countenances as they looked one to the other and then sped up the stairs to seek him out where he lay still sleeping. Hearing the laughter coming down through the open door was like the scent of challah on a Friday afternoon, sweet and doughy, warm with all the comfort of a day of rest. I remember that joy. I only pray that they will know that kind of surety and delight all braided together again.

I don't want any of this to be happening. I wake in the middle of the night and turn, expecting to find you there. But my Benjamin you are gone, gone. I am so angry at you for leaving me with this. You are off in some heavenly place arguing midrash to your heart's content, or playing chess, or rereading that treatise of Maimonides, the one you swore you would return to when there was more time for study. You left me. You left us here in this terrible upheaval. All of us trying to be so brave, trying and trying. I think you are a light in a dark room. I think you are a breath of wind rising up from the river and resting like dew on a stalk of wheat. I think you are a stone resting on your grave. Where are you? Where are you? Can't you hear me calling your name? Oh, my husband.

I wonder if maybe you hear me, and you are brokenhearted. I shiver at the thought of a blade cutting through your chest because I do know how much you loved us. I know that you held us dearer then anything. You must be in so much pain, if you are looking at us, knowing we are readying to take flight into some twisted version of the world you had no hand in creating.

Wait, that isn't true either. You did have something to do with it. Always the architect, even when others didn't know, you were laying plans. You organized the library into sections, just last year, so we'd know which volumes to save and which to let go to the fires. They will burn them; you and I know they will burn them. You made sure I had enough gold coin here at home. The jewels you began bringing home for the girls to have for their trousseau, you knew they would need them to run, now didn't you? Did you know this time was coming? I don't believe you would have left us if you knew. But then you always said to beware of a promise made by a king or queen. You said not to trust the words, to look beyond the whispers to the deeds. They wanted it all. They will oust us from here, erase us from their memories as if we never were, as if we did not give them what they needed to climb to the heights they have reached.

Of all those whispers, the breath of Torquemada was the one most rife with venom, you said. You never trusted him. Where are you now? Can you hear me? There is part of me that hopes you can, but still a greater part of me, the better part, hopes you cannot. I pray you are somewhere beyond any of this turmoil.

CHAVA

The box was square and fit in the cup of my hands. It was a puzzle box Papa brought me from one of his journeys to Granada. It was made of oak, ash and pine. There was a pattern of shapes that only hinted at how to take the box apart and gave no clue as how to put it back together. I was eight when he brought it for me. I spent all of an afternoon and much of the next day with it, until I could finally disassemble and then assemble it again. It was light, yet strong. Sarah had been given one of her own, but it was much simpler. It had only a piece to slide out and then it was easy to open and put back together again.

That next evening as we sat at our supper of eggs and rice, Mama asked what we would put inside the treasure boxes. Sarah said, right away, she would braid threads from her favorite dress and make a bracelet of them and put them in the box. Then she asked each of us if we would give her a strand of something we loved as well so she could weave it in with her own.

I said I would copy lines from my favorite psalms and verses as tiny as I could and fold them into little pieces and fill the box with ideas. I didn't ask anyone else to contribute their favorite words. The box always sat on the table by my bed. Over the years, I occasionally added a line from something I had read or a piece I worked to translate.

The day of the fête for Daniel's and my betrothal, I copied a line from Halevi's Poem of Love: Ever since You were the home of love for me/ my love has lived where You have lived. I gave it to him in the moments when our hands were clasped for the ceremony. I was just past my sixteenth birthday; he was turning eighteen. We were to be wed the following year. The verse felt so true to me. It had always been assumed we would marry. Ever since I can remember we had been paired together; our names woven into sentences about the future.

Then, last spring just before the Passover Daniel came to my house looking downcast and asked Mama if he might please speak to me in the garden. The first thing he did was to hand me back the verse I had given him. He took my hand and looked at me and said, "Chava, I no longer have a right to this." Before I could ask or interrupt, he continued. "My family decided to convert. It has been coming for a while and I am afraid, but we were forbidden to speak of it to anyone. They said we could still marry, and you could convert as well."

"Daniel," I interrupted, "why did you not come and talk with me before?"

"It is out of the question, is it not?" He still held my hand but did not look right at me.

"Why have you held this back from me? You will just walk away from me, from our promise?" I stepped back, pulling my hand away.

"I have been arguing with my father all week Chava. I would rather come to you and stay, with your family and our faith, as we have planned. He has forbidden it. He spoke with your father this morning. Your father is very angry."

Chava felt her own anger rise then, "As he should be."

"As you should be too, my love. But I cannot disobey my father." Daniel whispered, "I cannot." He stepped closer, reached for her hand, then dropped his to his sides.

"But you can leave me and break your oath?"

"They are all oaths Chava; I am now broken."

She felt pity for him then, sadness for them both and anger at everything. "It is not fair."

She leaned her forehead against his chin.

"No, it is not."

"Is there no way they will change their minds?" And then with a gasp, "Is it done?" She pulled herself back.

"No, it is not, and no they will not change. There is pressure from all of Papa's family. They want to convert all at once, so there will be no doubters."

"But why now? They say that Granada will fall within the year, certainly there will be rewards from the king for your father's work."

"My father does not trust Torquemada, the queen's confessor. He believes he will prevail upon the king and queen to renew the efforts of the Inquisition."

"My father thinks he will not be able to hold the queen's influence."

"Your father was always closer to Fernando, mine to the queen. She has convinced him our lives would be much better in the long run if we convert."

"What does that mean?" Chava asked.

"Unlike your family there has always been Conversos in mine. I just never thought it would be my own family."

"But Daniel, it must be more than that. Your father has never spoken of this before?" Chava could see her mother and her sister watching them through the window, giving them privacy yet keeping vigilance. She wondered if they knew. "You could break from them and be with us."

"I cannot leave my parents Chava, not after my brother's death. Perhaps we can find a way once things become calm again. Chava you do not know how this grieves me."

"And yet it is you who brings me grief, Daniel. You have wounded me more deeply than you can imagine." She bit back the angry words churning in her mouth.

"If you never speak to me again, I understand, but I will not give up on you."

"How could I ever speak to you when you will become one of them. Perhaps you will spit at us, call us Judaizers."

"Chava, never! You know I will never do anything but love you, even as I relinquish any claim to happiness with you."

"I have no choice it seems." She turned on her heel then and went into the house and rushed up the stairs. Sarah went to follow, but her mother told her to wait.

After a time, Chava realized she had put the paper with the script for Halevi's poem in her pocket. She smoothed it out and took apart the box, no longer needing to think of how she did it. She folded it and put it inside. Hearing her sister's footsteps on the stairs she wiped her eyes but began to cry again when she told Sarah. "Mama knew I think," Sarah said. "A note came via messenger from Papa. I think it was warning her."

April 10, 1492

Toledo

The key was kept separate from the chain where the keys to the house and her jewel box were kept. During her father's last trip to the south, her mother took Sarah and Chava aside and whispered for them to meet her by the cellar door just at the time when everyone in the household would be the busiest and they would not be missed. They went down the cellar stairs and through the second door they already knew was a secret heart of the house and then to the one they had not known about. Behind the heavy curtain, that suggested a solid wall, was another door and through that they entered. Esther struck a match against the firebox that was kept in the corner and lit the candle that was always kept there. In front of them and to their surprise were three trunks. Esther opened each to show them the manuscripts kept inside. These were all scrolls rolled tightly and banded with leather straps.

"These are very precious. Your father's family and my family have been entrusted with these for many years. They are some of the oldest writings we have."

"Who else knows of these?" Chava asked.

"Not many. Abravenel knows of course; your uncle and aunt; Isaac's family and now you."

"Does Isaac know?" Sarah whispered.

"His mother is telling him as well. We want to be sure all of you know what is necessary."

They hadn't spoken of the room and the scrolls since after their father died. But now during the preparations for leaving, it was brought again into to the conversation. "One of the reasons we want you to leave early is to take the most precious ones with you and assure their safe keeping. Others will go with Abravenel's children to Fez. There are some that have two copies.

April 11, 1492
Toledo

Chava went through each volume on the east wall in the library. She catalogued then placed them into piles: what needed to be stored, which were sent away before the final date of exile, and those that must leave with them to Portugal. After the ones stored in the secret room in the cellar these were the most precious of the manuscripts. The scribed works of Halevi and Maimonides, those first printed versions of the Talmud that arrived after Guttenberg had invented his press. There were also very old rolled manuscripts in Arabic, and one enclosed in a leather casing that was Greek. The old books in Hebrew and in Arabic were meticulously scribed and illuminated. Her family had been holders of many tomes for generations and amassed texts from as far away as Constantinople and Jerusalem and as close as the translation school in Toledo.

The draperies were open, and the windows unlatched to let in as much light as possible. The tapestry her father had purchased, just a few years ago in Ghent, hung on the opposite wall. The stitching was beautiful and fine. Chava paused to study it closely. It was the scene of a lady and a unicorn in a forest. Some of the trees had leaves appearing as if they were pages in a book. The colors were subdued but each element was so carefully worked that it felt as if a wind could begin to blow, or a unicorn could dart through the trees. Esther came in with a cloth wrapped around her head;

she had been working alongside Maria in the kitchen. "I love that piece as well, Chava. Should we think of your taking it to your Aunt and Uncle's?"

"I would rather think of you looking at it. Papa bought it especially for you. I think you should keep it here, at least for now."

Esther nodded, her gaze falling to the sorted manuscripts and books. "You have done so much just this morning."

"I have been thinking of it for days. Ordering what needed to be done in my thoughts, so when I started it was a matter more of moving each volume rather than deciding. I have been marking it all here in this ledger. I am afraid we will need to make a second pass through it all though."

"When we are a bit further along Don Abravenel and his son can come and we can all work together."

"Oh Mama, there is still so much to do."

"And we are doing so much. You keep working in the library if that is all right? Sarah will work with me in sorting our chambers. Do you mind?"

"I am best here I think."

"Do you need more help? I am sure one of father's assistants from the school…"

"Honestly Mama, I prefer to work alone. I can think better. It's as if I can hear Papa's voice." Chava's hand went to cover her mouth.

"Don't worry child, I often hear his voice, and often it advises me well. Though sometimes…"

"Sometimes? What were you going to say Mama?"

"Sometimes, it just makes me miss him more. It is hard not to have him; but now with all of this, it is harder."

"I know. I am trying…"

"Chava, you and your sister make it possible. Without you I don't know what I would do."

"But still, you are having us leave you. I can stay Mama…"

"No, we have talked about this. It is best for you to go now in these early days."

"Sarah can go with Isaac and I can stay and help."

"Chava, you are making me regret being so honest with you."

That stung Chava who prided her conviction to honesty over courtly propriety. "Yes Mama, I know. It's just…"

"I don't want to be apart from you either, but we will all rise to the challenge. I trust you to do that, daughter."

"Yes, I will. But still you would think the queen would not do anything that would separate families like this. Think of how she kept her children close."

"She does not mean to separate us, child. She wants us all to stay here and become loyal followers of the church."

"Like Daniel's family?" Chava stiffened as she said it. Esther drew her daughter in to a hug.

"You miss him still?"

"Always. But I have learned to put it away."

"And yet to carry it?"

Chava stepped back, returning to her questions about the queen. Her mother let the conversation about Daniel quiet, at least for now.

"But she knew Papa well enough and Don Abravenel and the others. How could Queen Isabel believe we would convert?"

"The queen believes one does what has to be done. She has set that example herself."

"But why does she believe Torquemada?"

"I do not have the answer to that, I hope that her majesty knows. Perhaps it has to do with her own past, all those years at Arevalo and her mother's illness. I am praying that will change."

"Do you really think so?"

"I can do no more than hope, then try in my way to make that hope come true."

"Be careful Mama."

"I am, we will talk more about this when Don Abravenel comes. Do you think by tomorrow afternoon we will be far enough along?"

"Let us hope so."

Esther kissed her daughter on the cheek then and left to return to the kitchen. Chava began to reach for another manuscript but turned to the tapestry. She stared for a long time at the depiction of the woman and thought, "There is something you know, lady. I believe there is something you know."

April 12, 1492

Toledo

All through Sarah and Chava's childhoods, there was a sense of plenty. There were always more books to read, more afternoons to ride, more lessons to learn. There was a sense of abundance even during the long stretches when their Papa was gone, when they missed him terribly, there was plenty to fill their time and days. There was plenty in the pantries. In the mornings bread roasted on a grate over the fire that it could be rotated by a handle that kept cool enough so you didn't even need a cloth or a glove but could just turn the contraption so that the bread would toast up perfectly golden on each side. Then be readily lifted out when it was done. Fresh churned butter sat in a dish on the wide planked table. Next to it, scooped into a small bowl was blackberry jam from the summer before. Milk steamed from the pitcher it had just been poured into. More bread was sliced and placed onto the toaster rack even as the girls spread their warm bread with butter and scooped jam on top. The milk was poured into their small earthenware bowls. They ate with the delight of all the flavors running together in scents and tastes, they knew there would still be more if they wanted it. Now, as Chava looked at the piles of what was to be packed away and what was to be taken she realized how it had all been stripped down.

Now, what remained were the essentials. The feeling of plenty was gone. Not much time, no more books, no more extra bolts of cloth that would become dresses, no more wool that would be woven into cloaks. What they had here, what they carried with them, would have to be enough. What there was least of all was time. Time to be in their home, time with their mother. The time with their father had already run out, gone before there had been enough. Chava guessed that from this time on she would always want more.

CHAVA

When we were small, Isaac, Sarah and I played hide and find. Often, we were joined by visiting cousins or another child from our household. I would start us with a story. "One day in the village there was a giant's footsteps heard and all the children, except for one, were told to go and hide and not come out until someone came to find them." Usually it was Isaac who would seek us out. But one day Juanito, Maria's nephew, was chosen

64

and we all scattered to hide. I ran to the garden shed and hid behind the door. Not such a clever place perhaps, but I did have the advantage of being able to see Juanito. He found me third, after Isaac and another cousin, but Sarah was nowhere to be found. Almost an hour had passed when we all became watchers and went in search of her. When another half hour had gone by with no sign of Sarah, we became frightened. I found Maria then who wiped her hands on her apron and followed me into the courtyard. She assigned each of us to a different area, but still no Sarah.

She said we would search inside then. I looked upstairs while the boys searched all the rooms downstairs. We looked behind chairs and under blankets, but still no Sarah. We began to shout her name then, just as mother came in the door. She demanded to know what was happening and what we had done to Sarah. My mother took my hand and told the boys to go with Maria into the kitchen to get their merienda of bread with honey and milk. Come with me, she said, and I followed her down the stairs to the storeroom. We had already searched there but not so carefully, it was dark, and we were not allowed candles.

My mother took a sconce from the wall and a flint from the shelf next to it and lit the candle, telling me to follow her. To my surprise, a door swung open onto a room I had never been in before. There on a small bench was Sarah sleeping. Mama put her fingers to her lips to hush me as I was about to yell and shake my sister. I began to cry, and Sarah sat up. My mother smiled. I hadn't let myself realize how scared I was at losing Sarah. My sister started to laugh at me but, realizing my tears were sincere, she came and hugged me instead. My mother closed the open door and said, "I will tell you both a story." She hushed my bubbling questions and told me to sit next to my sister. She sat on a stool.

"When this house was first built this was a passageway leading out and underground to exit onto a street leading below to the river. When your great-grandparents came to live here, they kept the passageway but dug out this room and lined it with cedar. Smell. Both Sarah and I sniffed in deeply then. She showed us how the walls, that seemed to be nothing but walls, pressed open to reveal cabinets lined with cedar. And how there was a false floor that allowed for more storage.

My mother said in a whisper, "This is our secret room. Like a secret chamber in your heart, it is where we can put what is most precious to us if the time comes that we must hide things. Sarah followed me down here one day when I was coming to check on something. That is how I guessed she had come in here to hide. No one else knows, just us and Papa."

"Not even Maria?" I asked. I was always told Maria was a trusted member of our household.

"Not even her." Mama assured me, "Sometimes it is best not to tell everyone everything. But now you know. It is a secret you must not tell anyone."

"Not even Isaac?" Sarah asked.

"No one", my mother said very seriously. She stood up from her stool and pushed it away and showed us how a floor board lifted. Below there were hidden handfuls of gold coins. We clamored to know if there was more. She told us yes, that it was always wise to keep some things hidden away. I demanded to know why. "The day your great-great-grandparents had to leave Montpellier, they were forbidden to take with them many of the texts that they had worked so hard to translate. And from the ones they had sold they were made to leave part of the coins they had been paid behind as well. To give them to the rulers, the ones who would take over their houses, and change the synagogue to a church and close the classrooms to our people."

"But why Mama? Who made them leave?" I had known from always that my mother's family had long ago come from France, from a city near the sea that had soft lights and that my family had been professors and translators. But I did not know they had to flee. It was the same story but told differently now. There was an edge of sadness to my mother's voice. But I also heard an edge of anger I had never heard when she told us about her family's old life in what she refers to as a softer place.

She admonished us never to hide there again unless it was her or papa telling us to go to the secret room. She said to be sure not to tell the boys where Sarah had been. She would tell them she had been asleep behind a sack of grain and we must not have looked too well. We giggled then thinking how we had put one over on the boys. She let us laugh. She closed the door with a special latch and as we came to the cellar stairs blew out the candle.

"Will you tell us more of the story Mama?" I asked.

"Yes," she said, "it is time you knew the whole story daughters. There is much to learn about what you do not know."

April 15, 1492

Toledo

The rain continued all day. As the sun set, the dark clouds caught the last rays and it appeared as if there were candles burning inside of them. The wind picked up and the unlatched windows blew back suddenly. Juan and Jose brought wood into the house and latched them firmly, making sure everything was tightly fastened against the incoming storm. The fires in the dining room and the library were banked. The girls and their mother sat in chairs pulled close to the fire in the salon. Esther asked Maria to fetch her shawl. It had grown suddenly colder as the rain fell harder. Another harsh rain from the northern sierra, unusual for these weeks of April.

Sarah sat almost motionless watching the flames. As people left synagogue the Saturday before they all stopped to talk about the edict. It was widely known that there had been attempts to persuade the king and queen with money and favors; more money, more favors. Many said it was the financial support from the Jewish community that had allowed them to win Granada. It was Jews that had first arranged the marriage between Fernando and Isabel. And now it would be Jews who were made to leave.

"Mama, what if it rains like this when we are traveling?" Sarah looked at her mother.

"Is that what you've been thinking of child? We will wait until after the worst of the rains have passed."

"No, I was thinking of Papa actually; of how he would have recounted some journey or crossing in a storm with laughter. All I can do is sit here and think about getting wet to the bone."

"We will be as ready as we can." Esther rose to poke at the fire. She did not want to have this conversation now, not on a night like this when you could hear the buffeting of the weather against the stones of the house.

She sat back down, "We will not speak of this now." Both her daughters looked at her, somewhat surprised. It was not like her to avoid a conversation. Still, they recognized the edge of loss in her voice. "Chava, take a candle and go to the library. Come back with something to read to us. Something with flowers; something that speaks of late spring."

"I know, Mama. I'll be right back." Chava went to the library and reached for the bound verses of Halevi, her father's favorite poet. He had sometimes worked translations for the poems the way a painter works at sketches in order to learn perfection. She remembered her father's response when she asked why he translated, "To rejoice in the words," he had answered.

She chose a bound manuscript in her father's own hand where he had copied poems into Hebrew and on the facing page, translated them into Castilian. "Here we are", she said when she came back. "Look what I have brought. Shall I read or do either of you want to?"

"You", they both said, "you read." And Chava recited, first in Hebrew and then in Spanish, alternating between the two as her mother and sister watched the fire and listened to the words that buffered the sounds of the storm.

She had chosen Halevi's poem of spring "… she pales the stars that have in heaven their dwelling...". Chava read until they felt quieted and were all tired, until the wind had lessened, bringing down just a light patter of rain.

Juan came in then to ask if there was anything else that was needed. He stood listening as Chava read. "Did you father write that?" he asked.

"In a way he did. It is his translation of another's words, but his own sense of them."

Juan nodded, "It must be like singing a song that someone else wrote. Your voice makes the words different, somehow finding a way to make them shine."

"Exactly" Chava replied. "Juan, I am glad that it will be you accompanying us."

"You know I will do my best to make sure you are safe. I will bank the fires. They are already well lit upstairs so your rooms will be warm."

"Thank you" they each replied as they rose to ascend the stairs. At the top, they kissed their mother good night. Maria was there to help Esther prepare for bed. The girls, as was their custom, would help each other.

After changing into their sleeping gowns and pulling back the quilts, Sarah touched her sister's cheek. "Can you imagine being gone?"

Chava replied, "I have been gone sister."

"No, I mean gone not to return, that this would no longer be our home."

"I imagine it all the time." Chava gave her sister a kiss on the cheek and turned over.

She turned back, "Sometimes it makes me angry, and sometimes sad; and at rarer moments, I wonder what there is to know, what we will discover."

"I just think of never being really warm again, never being really content."

"Go to sleep, it will seem less hard."

"For you maybe."

"For you too, Sarah. For you too." Chava fell asleep quickly and for once it was Sarah who lay awake watching the fire burn itself down.

CHAVA

I woke myself by yelling in my own dream, 'Get away, get away from me!" I don't know how Sarah was still asleep. I turned towards her right after I came awake. She looked quiet, as if she was dreaming of soaking in a hot bath scented with rose petals. Dreamy and quiet. I was filled with nightmares. The sound of small feet coming after me, small wrapped bodies, children but not children carrying clubs, beginning to strike me. I sat up in bed, moving slowly so as not to wake Sarah. I reached for my shawl against the cold outside of the blankets and quietly got up to relieve myself. I realized then that some of the noise I heard in my dream, the sounds of stones and hoof beats was actually thunder. I slipped the chamber pot back under the bed and crept down the stairs, feeling my way. I went to my window seat and sat for a long while watching the storm. The lightning cast an ominous glow on the tower of the church. At moments it lit the river further below; the sound of rain washing along the gutters of the street cleaning everything.

If it could only wash away the edict. Take away this new law that forced us out. Oh, I miss Papa all over again in that ripping way, like in the first days after he died. I leaned my head against the glass of the window to feel the rain and the wind and listen for his voice. But all I hear is a howling around me and the memory of my own screams waking me. It is cold, I am tired and so go back to my own bed. I slip into the room as quietly as

71

possible, crawl back under the blankets careful not to let the cold air reach Sarah. But she murmurs, "Where have you been?"

And I answer, "To see the storm."

She rolls back and then slides her back against mine for warmth, the way we always slept when we were little. Back to back. Looking out to our own separate worlds but connected in the warmth and comfort of our shared bed. I can barely remember a time when Sarah wasn't beside me. I was only two when she was born. There are glimpses of my mother round and full, of my leaning my head against her firm belly, of trying to sit on her lap but just balancing on her knees. I remember Sarah in the cradle. I rocked her and sang my own little songs to her. I did not mind her taking my place on mother's lap because then I spent more time with father. He would swoop in whenever I was about to fuss for mother.

April 17, 1492

Toledo

Today was not a day for meandering, not a day to take the longer path, it was a day to complete tasks. Today was a day for clouds to drift by as quickly as possible, for the sky to clear and the sunlight to be as brilliant as it could. It was not a day for questions, not a day for listless wonderings, not a day for anything but to do what needed to be done. It was a day to make a list of priorities and then to start at the top and cross them out one by one. It was a day of clocks, seconds ticking, hours marked, minutes counted.

There were bundles to be tied and things to be tossed, decisions to be made and losses accounted for. It was a day for carrying out plans. Not making new ones. A day for straight lines, for finding the shortest line between things, for calculations without any second guessing. No staring at the walls or imagining the shapes of branches for being anything more than what they were. Extensions of trees seeking out sunlight in the most expedient way.

It was not a day for pretending or humming anything more than what would keep you on task. It was not a day to ask questions, not a day to ask for stories. It was a day for lists, a pencil to cross out items, no erasures, no changes, no additions. None. Not one. It was a day that moved inexorably from early morning to late night, measured and set, bereft of nuance, lonely for shifts, aching for the space of wavering shadow, the dust of silences left from song. It was a day of ending one thing after another.

At the end of it, tired as she was, she could not fall asleep. She had been tossing, trying to convince herself that she would sleep, but gave up and lit the candle next to the bedstead. She didn't want to wake her daughters so decided against going downstairs. Instead, she rose and grasped her shawl from the bed stand, took the candle and crossed the room to the small desk. She reached below to the small shelf where she kept the key and opened the lock. Inside were a number of documents pertaining to the house and a number of her own bound journals. She had begun to keep journals when she was eleven or so, as a way of practicing her writing. There were a number of years when she kept them in different languages to discipline her hand to write left to right as well as right to left. One of the journals was from the time before she married and another kept intermediately after the loss of her children. A third, thicker book was begun when Chava was a few months old and continued through Sarah's childhood, recording their deeds more than her own thoughts.

It was the second she opened now. The last entry in it written before Chava was born, filled with hope and dread. She knew then that she could not bear the loss of another child and yet she was waiting to give birth in a few short weeks. She remembered the night she had written the entry. Benjamin was away at court and her mother was staying with her. The house was warm in the summer weather. She brought the candle close to the page and read her own words softly aloud to herself.

Here I am rounder than a melon, my skirts billowing out in front of me and still I cannot believe there is a child inside. I don't know if I am more afraid that the child will birth well, or that it will be born still. Of course, I hope the child should birth well, but I also want that it should live and thrive. Not like the last one who lived for months and then died anyway, leaving me, if possible, even more bereft then the ones before. But somehow, I am sure this one will live and be well. I am sure too that it shall be a girl and then I make myself afraid by my surety. But surely G-d cannot mean me to suffer more than I have. Oh, how vain that sounds. Certainly, others have suffered worse than I, much worse. To watch a child be killed, to watch a whole family slaughtered. I know those who have witnessed this. I know my small deaths are untarnished with suffering. And yet the weight of them wrenches me so. It has left me raw inside, and at times I feel turned inside out so that everything wounds me. Is it so much to want a child to thrive, to live and grow and learn all that Benjamin and I have to teach her? How can this be wrong to want to bring a sliver of grace into the world to catch the light. How can this possibly be wrong?

There was a stain on the page, and she remembered she had been crying. There was a page left blank, so she took up her quill and her ink jar and wrote:

It was worth it to have each of them near me for so long. I am so sorry I will not be by their sides when they have children, as my own mother was able to be by mine. It breaks my heart that I will not be there, but they will have each other and what strength I send them away with. And I will send them away with strength. They were only loaned to me by Yahweh and so what claim do I have beyond love? They shall carry that with them even if I am not there. Love will be with them.

Esther blotted the page then and finally, feeling tiredness and sleep descending, she closed the lid to the desk and went back to bed. Hanging her shawl on the bedstead she blew out the candle, pulled the quilts up over her and turned away from the empty side of the bed into sleep. She woke in the morning with a renewed sense of purpose, strong enough to outweigh and alleviate her tiredness. The sun was rising, setting the sky to a soft pink and lighting the towers of the highest buildings; the cathedral being the tallest of all. She had not drawn the curtains the night before, leaving them open so the light would awaken her as was her habit unless Benjamin had returned late. He would not return again; and so since his death, she had slept with the heavier curtains open.

She pulled the blankets back and as she did so, heard the door to her room open gently. Maria, always up even earlier then Esther, had brought her warmed milk. When she saw her mistress awake she set the small tray on the table beside the bed and Esther nodded a small thank you at her and then said, "Sit Maria, you and I must talk."

Maria turned to get the stool from where it stood on the other side of the room, but Esther told her to come and sit on the bed beside her. "You know the girls are getting ready to leave to go to their Uncle and Aunt's in Portugal?" Maria nodded her head and Esther continued, "If I were to say it is your choice to go with them or stay here with me, which would you choose?"

Maria looked surprised or at least feigned it. There was little that went on in the house that she was not aware of. "You are not going with them?"

"You know I am not." Maria smiled, faintly. "I have watched you watching as always. I am sorry I have not spoken to you before now but, to be honest, there was a piece of me that was pretending I was going with them."

"I think I knew it all along, mistress Esther. If it is my choice, I will stay here with you. I have lived in this household as long as you have. You are as much my family as anyone."

"Maria, if you stay what will your conscience say?"

"What do you mean?"

"You know what the decree has stated?"

"You know I cannot read and write very well."

"Maria, I believe you can write and read more than you let on…I know because I taught you. I know there is little you forget."

"Well then, mistress, perhaps this is true, but my first loyalty is to you."

"Beyond your loyalty to the church?"

Maria fingered the cross around her neck, "You have never asked me to give up my beliefs and I would never ask you to give up yours."

"I believe you, but what if your priest asks you if I am still a Jew; what would you say?"

"I would say you are a good mistress."

"Maria that might not be enough. If the date passes before I am able to complete my work you would have to lie. You would have to say I am a good Christian."

"You are a better Christian then many, Madam."

"Maria what if they put you to a test; what if they threatened to have you excommunicated from the church?"

"Then that would not be very Christian of them."

"Maria, do you truly understand what I am asking you?"

"More than you think, Mistress Esther. I understand more than even you think I know. Have your milk; it will be cold and then the girls will be up and there is much to do."

"What would I do without you Maria?"

Maria gave Esther's hand a squeeze then left the room. Esther drank her warm milk from the small bowl. She rose and pulled back the bed sheets and went to the basin where Maria had poured hot water and washed her face and hands. She said her own blessings, thankful for the company of someone she felt she could trust.

She dressed in simple house clothes and went down where the fires were already stoked in the library and the salon. Going into the kitchen she saw Maria had already set to work on a stew for dinner, cocido with chicken and lamb and garbanzos. The Catholics ate something similar but with pork and sausages. She remembered Maria instructing any new help to be sure never to buy pork that the family did not care for it. She trusted Maria to keep more than just the kitchen in order. She trusted her to keep her safe.

CHAVA

It seems the life I led before Papa's death and the threat of the edict was years ago and yet it was only months. For seventeen years, my days had a center. If not all the same, there was a rhythm to them and then the ground split open. Just last fall, I rose in the morning to the thought of daily chores and studies, to a temptation to sneak away down to the river, to the hope of going riding in the hours before dinner.

Now I wake and think which are the best books to take away? Have we catalogued each jewel, each coin? Do we know each stop we will make on the journey? Will we need to carry water or are the streams sure to be running? Question after question.

I want to sit lost in the verses of Halevi or the Songs of Solomon. I want to ride out past the fields knowing I will return to dinner at the table where there will be conversation that is not filled with the notes of goodbye. I want to wish away what is, to claim back what was. And then I think what if this moment, filled with planning, when goodbye has not yet been said, what if it is this very moment that I will be longing for when I am sitting at my aunt's and uncle's table and we are remembering our home?

I still cannot believe Mama will not come. She says I am badgering her, trying to wear her down. She's not wrong, but then I wish all the more that Papa was here because then we would lay out all the reasons to go or to stay and at least I would be sure the decision had been weighed fairly. Mama has been nothing but brave since Papa's death, nothing but kind to Sarah and me knowing how much we miss him. I know how much they conversed, weighing out decisions, and I want her to try to do this with me, but she cannot. She says it is her work to protect us and she is not yet so old that we are meant to protect her. There is no arguing when she has set her foot down. And yet, I keep trying to think of ways to change her mind. I am scared for her. Although, she does not seem frightened, rather she seems emboldened by the edict. I even heard her swear against the queen yesterday when she thought there was no one else in the room.

"Damn you to your hell, Isabel", she said. "You can damn me but there is no hell for me to go to. You have made it here already. I wish you are sent to yours for all the pain you have caused. Damn you to your hell. How can you have twisted the words of a kind and gentle rabbi to bring about so much grief and pain?"

Mama, I called out then, and she replied calmly as if she had not been speaking at all. "Chava, you are back from the market. Did you find the small bolt of cloth?"

"Yes, but it was only in a simple brown. I could not find the grays you asked for."

"Good enough, it is meant only to bind the things we want to keep together. It wasn't too dear?"

"No, Jaime gave me a decent price. He told me there are many who do not like what is happening to us. Tell your mother, he said, tell her she still has friends, she has always treated us fairly."

"I am glad to hear that, but I wonder how long until they are forced to say things they do not want to?"

"What do you mean?"

"We all have something we are not willing to lose, daughter. I am willing to defend my neighbors until protecting them means damning my own family. I don't know exactly, Chava. I know he means well, but I am afraid meaning well will no longer be enough."

"I heard you when I came in. I was not going to say anything, but I heard you. You are angry at the queen?"

"I am. Our family, many of our families have served her well. We helped her reach her dreams and desires. Helped her to marry in the first place. It was our community that financed the wars, our messengers that brought Fernando and Isabel together. But she has become emboldened with the power of her rule. She forgets what we did for her."

"Mama please, you must be more careful."

"She thinks she no longer needs us and so she is ready to throw us out. She perceives threat where there is none and she is acting from fear, not vision or love. Yes, I am angry Chava. I am very angry."

"Isn't it dangerous Mama? What if she heard you, what if someone heard you?"

"Then I would only be giving her reason to believe what she already believes. There is no changing her mind. I have spoken with Abravenel and with the others. They say she will not budge, at least for now. I think she still may come to realize the loss once her advisors are gone and there is only the empty sound of one voice in her chamber. At least that is the hope I am clinging to."

"This is why you are staying?"

"In part, yes. That one string of hope bet against everything that is ours. This is why I am staying and why you are going. It is barely a tenuous balance now, Chava. If your lives were part of the equation I could not bear it; I could not bear it at all."

"But they are Mama, it is all part of the equation. Either way you are subtracting us from your decision."

"No, no my dear, you at the very center of all my decisions. If I know you and Sarah are safe, then I can do what must be done to save our home. Not only our home, but our legacy. You two are the most important part of that legacy, but there are other things too." They sat then and Esther reached for Chava's hand. She placed her other hand below Chava's chin and raised her face, so her eyes were looking directly into her daughter's. "There is nothing, nothing more precious than your lives. Not a mass of gold, not jewels, not lands, not books."

"But words Mama, don't they matter? The manuscripts? Especially the old ones that are irreplaceable?"

"They matter, but nothing is irreplaceable except for a person. That is why I will stay for now and get out as many as I can, but I will not jeopardize your safety to do so."

"But you will jeopardize your own?"

"Only to a certain degree, Chava. I have assurances from others; there is a group of us as you well know. But no one will assure your safety. Just one from each family; that is what we have decided. At least we know each family will have a foothold out of Spain."

"So now I'm just a foothold, nothing more." Chava tried to laugh, but her eyes were cloudy from tears.

"Much more daughter, and besides do not forget you will be taking things with you as well. It is enough of a risk. Vague as some of the edict reads regarding what may be carried you are crossing the line of what is allowed. That is all I am willing to chance at this point."

"If there is no more arguing with you Mama, at least let me help more."

"Gladly, I have started that second sorting. Deciding exactly what goes to where and rechecking the ledger."

"How are you deciding what goes where?"

"For now, as much by weight as content, that is the pile to go to Fez. That one to Salonica where the Sultan Bayezid has sent invitations and that one to Poland, where the king is graciously asking us to come. Those will go to Amsterdam."

"You'd think we were book sellers."

"It is what we are for now, Chava; keeper of words, holders of ideas. If not, they will disappear to flame and ash I am afraid."

"I miss the times when I would hear the arguments of ideas coming out of this room. Do you remember Mama?"

"How could I not? Muhammad and Chaim, Jakob and your father and even Father Jose, they could turn one phrase for hours. Did you know the king himself would argue with your father sometimes? He would call him into his chamber and say, 'Tell me Benjamin why did G-d make Job fight so hard?'"

"And what would father say?"

"He told me he answered the king by saying, 'Why do you make me work so hard my Lord?' And the king looked at him quizzically at first and then he and your father laughed. And Papa continued by saying, 'Are you assuring yourself how much I love you your majesty? Or is it that you think I like the challenge?' And then the king told him to sit and have some wine with him."

"Was father friends with King Fernando or did he only serve at the king's pleasure?"

"Kings have no real friendships daughter. But I suppose he was one after a fashion. The king trusted him at least."

"Then how could he be making us leave?"

"I do not know. Torquemada has Isabel's ear and she has the king's. We are only secondary to any plans they have. We have become an irritant instead of a help. We will have to wait and see, they may yet change their minds."

"Or maybe Torquemada will fall off a cliff."

"Hush daughter, you could be taken for less."

"From our own home, who would tell?"

"It seems these days that the walls are growing ears. Now come help me bring down these books from the higher shelf. Then go and wake your sister for the morning is growing as old as me."

"Ah Mama, you are not so old as you think. Not to me."

"But it is not your eyes that worry me daughter."

"Whose then?"

"Only Yahweh's."

"Well to him you are nothing more than a child." Chava retorted.

"You, my girl, have your father's wit. Now let's see if you have his prowess at book selling as you say. Get those books down. I'll go wake Sarah myself."

ESTHER

I remember the first steps Chava took. She rose up from a squat and stared straight ahead, took a breath, frowned for a moment and then setting her mouth in the way she still does when she's determined about something, took five steps toward the chair she had set her sights on. She fell and rose and took five more steps. There was a book on the chair and when her hands touched its cover she laughed. Her father scooped her up then and put her in his lap and read to her from the book. She was just under a year old then.

Within a few months, I was pregnant with Sarah. At last we felt like a family. I remember the births of each of my children clearly. I can also remember their deaths though I covered the pain with a fog of love for those who remained. The little gravestones in the cemetery would never slip from my memory but they were no longer in focus. The other child I knew I had lost, before there was anything to mark him, was no longer a hollow. Now it was Chava's and Sarah's laughs that filled me.

I could still see the pity in other women's eyes even after Sarah thrived. The fact was that we had no living sons, but I didn't care. I had two daughters and they were curious and strong. If Benjamin longed for a son to take with him to temple, to chant with him, he did not say so to me. He only told me how glad he was that our daughters were so bright. He taught them right from the start to read and to write, to chant the prayers and to add and cipher. He knew to count his blessings and I did not need to be reminded.

When you have buried children, when you have felt their lifeblood course away from you, you cherish the warmth and energy that emanates from those that live. I conceived six times, only my two daughters grew into adulthood. My son died within a week of his birth and the other child I lost too soon to know if it was a boy or a girl. Too soon to know but not too soon to forget. That was the second child, a year after I lost Gabriel who we had time to grant a name but not even time enough to have a bris. His loss felt monumental; I had carried him with such love and hope. When I became pregnant soon after, I was filled with fear and with the knowledge that conception can bring as much hurt as joy. When I began to bleed at four or five months I was sent to my bed, but it didn't help. That child too left me in a river of blood, and yet another son lost soon after.

Then there was Chava, thank G-d for Chava, and then my little Sarah. My daughters grew and grew. After Sarah, I became more cautious. I waited to conceive but then I didn't. My husband was always loving to the girls, never acting as if he missed a son, but I know he did. He missed the two that we lost.

I am not sure if this makes it easier or harder to say goodbye to them. I have known greater loss then watching my daughters leave. I have cast dirt into a grave from which a child will never again see light. My daughters are walking into the long afternoon sun. They are walking toward the great expanse. They are walking in to the rest of their lives. If I am not there so be it. Someday, someone will write of these dark times when we are being thrown from our home for centuries yet again. Cast into wind and buffered up against mountains, made to cross waters and settle yet again with those who had been cast out before and found their way to some far off place.

My daughters will tell their daughters and sons, they will write it down. Someday my great-great-grandchildren will know this house in Toledo, as if the stairs and stones had echoed their own footsteps. My daughters know the travails of Jonah and the greatness of Moses and that was thousands of years ago. We are a people that carry our stories. Our history is as close as if it were this morning's bread. And we take our sustenance from it.

Chapter Five
Passover

April 1492
Toledo

CHAVA

When I was little, I would help Maria tend the garden, pulling up weeds and carrying the early greens, in a basket that was just my size, into the kitchen. As I got older, I was sent to the baker's around the corner. Our chores were close to home- the garden, the baker, the shop that sold Sabbath candles, the ever present daily work of keeping a home. We always helped in the kitchen and the house. Mama wanted to be sure we knew what went into running a home. It was also her way of assuring how much work was done on our behalf and that we knew we were fortunate. Our lessons were no different than our chores. They too were part of our days. We learned letters and ciphering; we learned languages and embroidery. We learned to translate. We learned to ride and care for the horses. I was left with just enough time for daydreaming out my window seat. Though really, I was supposed to be practicing my needle work or my letters. Curving the Arabic script on the wax boards. Letters came easily enough to me, but needle work didn't come at all. I gave up quickly, never quite understanding why my fingers could make a stylus form whatever shapes I willed. But they could not make even a leaf, let alone the stylized buds that Sarah made with such ease.

Chores and lessons filled our days. There was no end to them and no beginning. They made the rhythm of our life: drawing water, gathering herbs, learning new words, drawing columns on our wax boards, moving between languages. It was all part of the same set of laws that guided us. We were told that every deed is a prayer made manifest. You are the sum of what you do in the world, and if we did it with love our lives would be rich. Mama used to say making honey is the work of bees; they are at it all the time. Just look at the gold they make to share with us and how it makes everything sweet.

But the chores for Passover were special. Numerous as they were, they were my favorite. Of all the holidays it is the one I loved the most. It is so full of stories and songs. Preparations start weeks in advance. The cleaning and clearing out of all the winter things as the days grow lighter. Sweeping every kitchen shelf, making sure there were no hidden crumbs forbidden during the eight days of Passover. And as we worked, we sang, at least in other years we did. Mama passed a feather into every corner to clear any last bits of leavened bread. Everything that was not kosher for Passover was sold to Maria's family for a half penny coin. In the last days, before the Passover, every drop of hametz was taken from the house and burned. Everything was made new.

The Passover story, though it had its share of pain and trials, had always left me joyous. I held the image of a sky full of stars pointing toward our one true home. Miriam's hiding her baby brother, but never letting him out of her sight. The way Moses stood in front of the Pharaoh and demanded that his people be released. Even the first born deaths, the hardships of the slaves, the desperation of Moses when he first fled, all of this paled in comparison to the act of rising up and seizing freedom. The swoosh of the Red Sea parting and then of Miriam's tambourine catching a glint of fire as she raised it up in song once they had left the armies behind.

This year, even before we knew the words of the Alhambra decree, I could not summon up the joy. I will miss Papa's baritone on the prayers, his voice praising me when I raise a question or tell a story of my own. Daniel's conversion haunts me still. I remembered the happiness of last year's Seder; that song and laughter was now a distant echo.

The edict casts a shadow. It makes it easy to dwell on the dark side of Passover's story: the persecutions of the Hebrew slaves, the plagues brought down on Pharaoh, the deaths of the firstborn sons, the marks of blood above the door, the wide wings of the angel of death.

Passover, so close to Easter, has always been a time when the blood libel stories seem to come again. The old falsehood telling how Jews used the blood of Christian children to make their this missing, as happened just two years ago, someone would be sure to stand accused. Sometimes a priest or a family member could quell the lies, but sometimes they did not. Sometimes it did not serve them to, or perhaps they didn't have the power over fear. We all knew the stories of how Jews had been attacked in England, France, and in our Spain. Not once or twice, but many times. Jews were burned when the child in La Guardia had gone missing. And even after they found the boy, they still claimed it was our fault.

I thought exiles and diasporas had faded into history like the tales of giants or horses with wings. Something that had once been true, but the facts changed in the retelling of the tale. But this is not a myth, not a legend, it is our lives. I know they are still trying to convince the king and queen to reverse their decision, but there is only a small chance. It feels as if the rains will bring no flowering this year, only mud, as if the sun will choose to hide itself, and the tips of green, the heralding of hope will drown. When the Israelites had their exodus, they were fleeing slavery and walking toward freedom. We are leaving what we thought of as freedom, only to be driven into exile. I am weary today, just weary of it all. Mama must be even sadder than I.

The invitations to Seder are sent. The special plates and glasses that we keep just for this holiday are made to shine, the special wine cups from Venice glitter. Mama insisted that while we will have less people in attendance, we make it beautiful all the same. Papa would have wanted it so. But sometimes what is beautiful can make you sad as well, because as it opens the heart to let in joy, the heart is opened to grief.

This morning of the first Seder is the first time in a week that my head is not filled with lists of what to take and what to leave. Every other morning I wake with the words of goodbye on my lips, the image of my mother slipping from my embrace. But today I woke thinking of the table setting and the food preparation, the scent of roasting lamb, leek soup simmering on the fire and the sound of chopping dates and walnuts for the charoset. I could visualize the Seder plate laid with all the symbols of the holiday.

It was as if there are two rooms in my mind. One room is filled with leaving and the other filled with Passover. I shut the door and drew the curtains on the room of leaving. I decide very purposefully to remain all day in this room, filled with my favorite holiday at home and all the years we celebrated it happily. I quickly washed my face in the basin and put on clothes for working in the kitchen. But when I enter, I see Mama huddled at the corner of the table in deep conversation with Isaac's mother, both of them grasping the other's hands. They do not even notice me come in. Seeing them so worried furthers my resolve to keep the door on our leaving shut.

Isaacs's family will join us and our neighbors with their young children. Old Uncle Gael will come; he never married, unless you count the Torah as a bride. The children will make the meal lively, even if the rest of us are somber. They will ask the four questions; I'm sure they will laugh as we used to when we hunted for the afikomen. They are too young yet to truly understand what is happening. The baker will have the matzoh by noon as promised. His own will be the last out of the oven, still warm by the time he sits at his own Seder table.

I think of my mother staying after we leave and how the memory of our footsteps will sound the empty halls.

It is the first time I think that leaving might be easier than staying. Mama and Isaac's mother look up and move just a bit away from each other. My mother smiles, a bit crookedly, but still she smiles. Isaac's mother says, "We were planning out the last details of tonight's menu and decided we should have the dessert made of orange and almonds you always loved as children. What do you think, Chava?" I sit down next to them. Close up I see the lines marking my mother's face. She is more drawn then I had realized. I push an escaping curl back under her kerchief. I tell them the dessert sounds perfect and smile.

The women laugh and I wonder how long they have been sitting there together. I wonder how often they will sit together in the future when we are far away. How strange to think of yourself being mourned. How strange all of this is. I start to open the door to that maze of rooms, that labyrinth of leaving, but I pull the handle and shut the door once again. I ask what needs to be done next.

As evening approaches, the table looks beautiful. Early spring flowers set in small vases smell of the wind of the sierra, two sets of bees' wax candles stand tall in the silver candlesticks from our grandparents. At each place a small inscription from the book of Exodus. This had been my morning's work. The linen cloth covers the long stretch of table; it has tiny stitching done by nuns in the convent of Santo Domingo el Antiguo.

When they first came to Toledo our family bought linen from the convent. The purchase of cloth was a gesture of good will. Muslims, Christians and Jews traded goods and ideas. My mother said the other day that she was grateful neither her parents nor my father's were alive to see another exile. They thought Toledo would be a haven. But then I think my great grandparents' parents thought the same of Montpellier and of Sevilla. So many died and all were banished. It was one of the only times I saw my mother weep as she ran her hands against the linen. Old, yet still white, still cared for, and then I had a pang of fear. Who would care for my mother? Who would be here for Isaac's parents if there was no returning?

The Haggadah, the one we kept just for Passover, was handed down from my father's great grandparents. The binding still held true; the illustrations still shown brilliant in their blues and golds. We will pass it around the table to take turns reading the story of Exodus. I thought again that this was our first Seder without Papa presiding, and the last we would have at home. How could this be, first and last folded together in the same story?

All was ready: roasted lamb and eggs, the earliest spring greens and a dish of roasted root vegetables left from winter, sweets made of almonds and honey, and the soup that mama always made herself, passed down from her great grandmother, the way they made it in France.

The Seder plate was arranged in the middle of the table: lamb shank, roasted egg, parsley, salt water, charoset, and bitter herb. We were pleased with our efforts. Passover Seder felt like a reprieve from our own preparations for leaving, and yet it was the same story. It could be no accident that the edict came now as we took turns reciting our ancestors' exile from Egypt to search for a promised land.

Always at our Seders, after the traditional story of Moses, the plagues, the handing down of the holy law, the long wandering, we recounted the stories of the exoduses that had affected our own families. The exile from France, from Andalusia, and Isaac's family leaving England long ago. This morning Mama asked me to speak after the tellings of the past diasporas and relate the plans for our leaving. Your Papa would have asked you to she said when she saw my doubt. I held my chin up then and said I would. All those leave takings we have endured, not out of choice, but survival. I wonder though, survival, is that not also a choice?

This year, before we begin the prayers and the story of Passover, we say Kaddish for father. It is not ritual, but we make it our own honoring our father and how he so loved Passover. As we finished the prayer, Sarah leads us into one of the old songs. It was one of Papa's favorites, one about crossing into Sepharad as we called Spain. Then Mama says the blessing and lights one set of candles, Sarah and I light the other set together as we have done since we were small. When she bends near the flame and closes her eyes, I catch a glimpse of her as she must have looked when she was our age. I imagine her in her father's library, her fingers running along a page, and my heart swells with love for her.

We conducted the Seder so tenderly, more quietly than I can ever remember. Mama asked Isaac to begin the telling this year. It felt so strange; I could hear Papa's voice, resonant with joy, when he would begin to read from the Haggadah. Isaac tried to bring that sense into his own voice and began to read, "Many years ago in the land of Egypt." We each told part of the story and we passed the Haggadah round. As was tradition in our home, we took the passage we were given and embellished it in some way. Sarah would always have a song to add.

Papa used to have a poem and so I had been careful to choose one this year as well. It was a poem by Solomon Ibn Gabriol that I knew Papa loved well, "at morning and at evening I seek You/ I offer you my face and outspread palms/ For you I yearn, for you I turn your grace to earn" Mama smiled at me even as I saw her brush away tears with her fingertips.

I stitched the evening into memory even as it was happening. I stretched out each moment assuring that I could carry it with me. The youngest child began the questions and then we chanted it all together, "Why is this night different for all other nights?" We told the story of Exodus and we said the blessings. As always, when we counted out the plagues, we dipped out littlest finger in the wine and spilled a drop on our plates. We took our time and shared stories of other Seders. We included our father in each part of the Seder as he had always included us. Not until after the children had found the afikomen and received their reward, only when our ancestors had Zion in sight, did we begin to talk about our own impending exodus.

Of all our family and friends, we would be the first to leave Toledo. Others were still deciding exactly when to leave and even where to go. Some holding out hope that the king could still be swayed, whether by money or morality. I shared the plans for our journey and named the families we would visit on our way to Portugal. The little children had fallen asleep by then, but no one wanted to leave. Isaac asked if any of us knew of Colon's upcoming voyage, seeking a route to the east by sailing west. He had heard that Fernando and Isabel would finally approve the funds for his voyage and that Louis Santangel would help to finance it. Even though he was a Converso, he was still trusted by the royals. His money very dear to them as well.

There were rumors that Colon was readying his voyage to search for a promised land. Rumors that he too came from a family of Conversos who never really gave up being Jews. It was even said that some might convert in order to go with him to a land that would be beyond the reach of the Inquisition. But we were only going to our Aunt and Uncle's in Oporto. Although we were not sure for how long. It was likely that Portugal could follow the example of Isabel and Fernando and oust its Jews as well. But at least it would give us time to really make plans.

I know Sarah clung to the same hope as Mama, that we would only be gone temporarily. Like the great uprisings in Sevilla that drove our great grandparents to leave there and come to Toledo, this would be another passing wave. But I did not think so. There was something calculated in the way Torquemada was planning this; the way in which the Conversos had been challenged in recent years and the Jews left alone and now he turned on the Jews saying they were influencing the Conversos. It was designed to plant fear and distrust. Now that Spain is unified again they want a pure Christian nation. How quickly the golden age is forgotten. The schools of learning, the medicine and mathematics that were shared with the countries to the north, all came from the Muslims and Jews sitting together and then sharing with the Christians. It all came through the translators. What unified country do they think they will have when they remove from it the parts that think and sing and write and count the stars?

I know if my thoughts could be heard, I would be burned at the stake for heresy. And as a Jewish woman, I would be considered a threat to the king and queen themselves. My father warned us against Torquemada, a man angry at the world and angry at G-d. There is nothing I know of to appease his anger. He will seek to destroy. And so he has, with the blessings of the royals, turned against us. I do not believe they want our souls to be saved; they just want us to be gone. It was past midnight when our guests left. For the only time I could remember, we left the table just as it was and went up to bed.

The second day of Passover brought a quiet lull to the house, the cleaning done from the night before the preparation for the second night so much easier. It would be just the two families tonight, Isaacs's and ours. I came upon Sarah, sitting in the library with her sewing in her lap, staring at the fire. Sarah was quiet, usually she sang or at least hummed as she stitched.

"What is it sister?"

"Even my fingers are tired this morning, thinking of the road leading only away, there will be no coming back. Have you known Queen Isabel to ever change her mind?"

"I don't know." I thought about how much influence our mother had over our father.

"You are thinking of how Mama always swayed Papa, aren't you?" There was never much I could hide from Sarah. As much as I liked to see myself as the older sister, I knew how much she took in as she watched and listened.

"As always, you are right," I saw a smile coaxed out of her sadness.

But then she looked down and back up as if she would cry, "Oh Chava we will be orphans."

"We will never be orphans, not like that. We have each other; mama will write; we have aunt and uncle."

"We will have no parents at our weddings, perhaps we will never wed."

"Oh you will, and I know to who…" It was no secret to me that she and Isaac had eyes for each other. I was trying, as I had always done, to tease her out from the doubts that could sometimes settle on her so easily.

"Chava, talk to me. Do not try and change the subject."

I sat down next to her and we did talk, about how much we would miss the house and mother. All the time I was thinking there is no use to this. I will just carry it with me. There is no use in going on and on, but it seemed Sarah needed to do this; to make a list of what she would miss, and she didn't often ask. We talked the rest of the morning in whispers. By the end she felt better, and I felt worse. "I am going out for a ride." I stood up and declared suddenly, "I need the wind to shake this off me!"

Sarah laughed then and said, "You and the wind, there is a part of you that will be quite happy on the road Chava." I kept my smile to myself and thought my sister knows me well.

On the second night of Passover, we gathered in the salon holding warmed cups of mulled wine. The afternoon had carried rain and the cold could still be felt when the sun did not show. By seven o'clock, we were seated at the long table in the comedor, the Seder plate at the center. The plate of matzoh was next to it. Tonight, it had been decided we would remember Spain, our Jerusalem of the west, our golden land that had grown tarnished. It was never truly gold but brass we said, strong and shiny, but only when it was kept polished.

Because of the close ties to the court that our family's and Isaac's had the community believed their presence, along with some other key families, would be a constant reminder to the court of what they were losing by banishing the kingdom's Jewish families. They were all politically astute to the workings of the court and knew it might be possible that they would have to feign the beginning steps of conversion. Even though they feared that the appearance of considering converting could be dangerous, leading others to think it was really an option. It would be the work of the elders to spread the word carefully.

They had rehearsed this, even saying that those who were leaving were going to talk with other family to convince them as well and they would be back. But those not so attuned to the politics and whims of the court, might actually convert. What else could be done though? Abravanel and Seneor had tried to reason and then coerce the king and queen with more money than he had ever before been offered. Thirty thousand gold coins is what we were told. But Torquemada entered just then and raised his voice to the king and queen, reminding them that Judas had sold their lord for a price.

The king looked to the queen and she said no. He followed suit. But for a moment they had seen Fernando waver and so they believed he could change his mind and convince the queen to change hers. A sliver of a chance that the edict would be lifted, and Spain would remain our Jerusalem, tarnished perhaps, but still home. It is amazing how large a sliver can seem when it is the only light in the room.

ESTHER

The hidden cellar was here when we came to the house. It was lined with cedar. The house belonged to a Converso family that left after a wave of hatred had washed over Toledo. They were cousins of cousins. I suppose we all are somehow. When Benjamin's family came from Sevilla, they stored manuscripts and some other precious things in this cellar. They lived openly as Jews and so much of what was in their everyday lives was kept upstairs in full view of everyone. But hidden here were things that were precious, priceless. They kept them secret to all but a few. Scrolls that had been entrusted to them, writings and records. We have been adding to that store as we sort through the library. But there is a fear in me that this room will be found, that this time there will be much more thorough searching. Sometimes I must admit I find myself wavering, perhaps I should leave with them. I am not feeling so steadfast in my conviction as I let on. Surely there are others I can entrust with ensuring the safe passage of these manuscripts and artifacts.

Ah, if only Benjamin were here. He could see me through this. I try to imagine what he would say. We sought each other's counsel on things and gave each other comfort when there was no counsel that made sense. Still he kept some things from me as is the wont of men. Things of the court, things of the study house, those conversations would serve me well now. I am trying to conjure them up so I can take advice from the dead, before we all have joined them.

CHAVA

Once when I was seven, I trailed after Isaac and his brothers. Sarah was just young enough to be at home asleep for the siesta. I followed them down to the river and then along the bank. They came to a place I had never been before. There were stones that you could cross out to a small island. I followed them across the first few until they looked back and saw me and yelled at me to go home. "This is no place for a girl", Jacob, Isaac's older brother, yelled.

Well that got me mad and I jumped further than I thought I could, but when I came to the edge of that third ledge and looked at the river water rushing quickly between an even grander space, I froze. "I choose to stay here," I yelled across at the three boys. "I will stay still and keep watch for you."

Isaac, who knew me best and was just a year older, came back for me. He jumped effortlessly across, the water was deep and fast. When I jumped from the rock before, I had come to the edge and wet my feet enough to realize how cold it was. "Come," said Isaac, "we will cross together."

"No," I answered. "I'll stay here and wait."

"We will be gone a long time. They have a stash of fishing line there and we will not be back until dusk. If you are not coming, then you best go home." I walked back to the crossing point, but I froze. I came back again the other way and froze again. I was stuck. Isaac put his arm around my shoulders. "Chava, you have to go one way or the other; the currents come in and the rocks will be covered. You will get soaked or swept in." My eyes must have gone black with fear. He held my hand and said, "You jumped this once and you can do it again. I will stand here and watch.

"No, no you go on. Let me alone."

He sat down then, and I crouched next to him. "I'm scared. What if I fall in?"

"I'll jump in and get you."

"I don't want you to watch. It makes me more nervous."

He laughed then. "You can do it; you always manage."

I got up and turned quickly and ran for the edge, but it was as if I had turned to stone. I could not make myself do it.

"Close your eyes and just jump. It is no further than it was before."

But suddenly the water sounded so loud and the river seemed to taunt me. I thought I saw a snake. And then I saw Isaac begin to look at me in a way he never had. As if I were any girl and I screwed up my courage and ran and jumped back over. I turned and waved to him with a smile. I hoped he did not see how forced it was. When I got back to the shore, I sat and wept on the bank. Then I dipped my hand into the water until it ached with cold. I wanted to remember.

I had managed to get across on pride alone. I had to swallow my fear and now it felt like bile in my throat. I spit. And then, sure that the boys could no longer see me, I crossed all the way to where I had been and came back again. I did not get any further, but I made it back on courage instead of fear and pride. I felt like that little girl again, the river rising moment by moment.

April 22, 1492

Toledo

On the third day they began to put away the things brought down from the higher cupboards: Elijah's cup, the platter that held the matzoh, the Seder plate. They carefully dried each thing with a special cloth then wrapped it in others, stacking one on top of the other, readying them to be placed on the uppermost shelf. Just as Sarah turned to fetch Juan, to have him climb the small ladder to put the things away, she stopped. "What's the sense of this? There will be no next year."

Chava answered, "I don't know. I think Mama really believes we will back home again.

"I do not."

"Which Sarah, believe it will pass or believe Mama thinks it to be so?"

"I do not think that she believes. I think she is trying to put on a brave front for us so we will go and leave her behind."

"No, I heard her speaking with the others. She said instead of next year in Jerusalem, we should stay next year in Toledo."

"Yes, that proves it to me even more."

"What do you mean, Sarah?"

"It is an expression, a beseeching; no one really thinks that any of us will see a next year in Jerusalem."

"You think she really believes this was the last Pesach in this house?"

"Yes, I do. I am not sure if I believe it, at least not yet. But I think that Mama does."

"Sarah, you need to tell me more. Why is it you believe, and Mama does not?"

"Because my sister, I choose to believe, but our mother knows better. She also knows that you will not want to leave her behind and so she pretends."

"And why are you telling me this now?"

"I want you to prove me wrong. I want you to tell me that it isn't so, that she truly thinks we will return, that the king and queen will lift the expulsion." Sarah stepped closer to Chava.

"I don't know if I can. My surety is not so steadfast. I want Mama to come with us, and yet I understand her reasons for staying here."

"I want you to convince me we are doing the right thing. If you did not think that, how could you leave so easily?"

"Easily, how can you say that? I feel like we have been through the ten plagues. I feel like we have given the court every chance to change their minds and they have not."

Sarah gave her sister a hug. Chava swallowed to check the break in her voice. "I do not feel like there is really a choice. You know I argued with Mama?"

"I did not know, but I thought as much." Sarah sank onto the step of the small ladder feeling the hard wood beneath her.

"I begged her to let you and Isaac go, to let me stay with her. I begged for her to come with us. I said we can all go and then return. I said…"

"And she said no, to everything?" Sarah looked up.

"She said no to everything." Chava nodded.

"Then I will pretend I believe her. It will give her some peace of mind. Can you do the same?"

"I will try." Chava bent and put her hand on her sister's cheek.

"I dreamt that Mama gave me the key to the cupboard and sent it with us to Portugal."

Just then Esther came in, "Girls we will put the things downstairs in the chamber. There is no sense in putting them back this year. Take the Haggadahs out and wrap them well to put in the box with the cedar chips. They will go downstairs as well." The girls looked from one to the other and nodded.

Chava kept the Haggadah that her father had always used, the oldest amongst them, the one with the best illustrations and most beautiful lettering. She took it upstairs and put it with the things she would pack to take with them. As if she could carry her father's voice. As if she could wrap all the years and all the holidays into a small package. As if she could somehow keep them safe.

CHAVA

In the past week there have been as many different rains as days. A thunderstorm, a chaperon, that shook the house and woke us all. The next morning, after the fog cleared, it began to rain again, but softly, a fool's mist, a gentle rain, water suspended above water. It was the kind you hardly feel and yet it soaks you through and through. That night it dribbled and the next day was a constant thrumming against the cobbles. I watched the drops roll down the window panes.

I am tired of the wet and the thought of setting out in this weather has dampened my spirits even more. We have pushed back our leaving by a few days, waiting for the sun to begin to dry the roads. Hoping not to have to ride in the wet weather, cloaks soaked, progress slowed by mud and overflowing streams.

Maybe I should be more welcoming of the rain, as it grants another day before we leave. Or perhaps mother will just send us out into it as she had done when we were small children and days of rain had kept us too long inside. When our voices grew loud and we could no longer contain ourselves, even in the hallways or on the steps, she would open the door that led from the kitchen out to the small gardens and say go. Leaving off our shoes and sending us out in old clothes, she would have us look for worms or search out stones. Once we had grown up, she confessed she could not abide the noise we raised when the rains trapped us inside. When we came in, muddy and wet, she'd have a hot tub of water pulled near the kitchen fire, strip off our clothes there and then. She ducked us into the warm bath so we would not catch chill and so there would be no mud to track through the house.

Our mother always had us running more than other little girls we knew. Well not the little girls that had to work for their bread; they ran all the time, but the girls of other families like ours who knew to sit so much better than us in a prim, fastidious way. Then again, they could not translate passages the way we could, nor mount a horse, nor jump a ditch. Perhaps all the time mother and father were readying us for this. Though they could not have known the edict would come. They wanted to assure we would be able to set out on a road and make our way. That we would possess skills as well as courtly manners. That we would know how to carry ourselves, whether on a horse, in a village, or in front of the royal family.

At least we will leave by horseback. At least we have not been conquered by soldiers striding though our homes and taking what they want. We will leave with some sense of pride still, some sense of choice. Even if it is a choice we have been forced to make.

When I was eleven, Papa showed me a special way to breathe. He said it was another way to pray. Papa had just returned from a trip to Tangier where he had been with friends who study the Kabbalah. Papa studied when he was younger, but he traveled so often for the court that he no longer could spend the necessary time devoted to studying the texts he so loved. He told me I was too young yet to understand much of what they had discussed about these special writings, but he had one thing he could share with me now. That was sitting and breathing quietly, repeating a string of words, like a prayer. It was a way to pay attention and not be swallowed by all the other thoughts prancing around my head. Prancing, I laughed, like horses.

We practiced every day using different prayers and songs and even strings of numbers. He wanted me to see that even if all I had were numbers to count my breath, I could still calm myself and focus. Remembering that now, I think I must take the time to do that. To sit for a few minutes and focus and not be swept up in the swirling fears and worries.

But it is hard not to fall into the tumult. Neighbors come by to ask advice from Mama and she tries to give each person her best consideration, but I can tell it is tiring her out. I want to yell; don't they remember it was just a short time ago that they watched her sitting Shiva? It is not so long ago that she was raw with grief. It is not so healed that every request rubs against it and opens it again. But when I tell her to let me answer the door, she says, "It is my duty child, my responsibility, mine, and the Rabbi's wife, and a few others who have always served as leaders in the community. If you are a leader, that comes with some privilege, but it also comes with much responsibility. You cannot set it aside when you are tired or when it suits you. What would you have me do Chava, turn them away?"

I said, "No, just send them to Rebecca or Judith." And my mama put her hand on my shoulder, looked at me and said, "Don't you think their doors are opening and closing as much as mine?" I wanted to say, but they have not just lost a husband! I wanted to say they have more children and sons to help them. We are only three and we are tired and sore. But I knew it would have no merit. And I knew my mother was strengthened even as she felt tired.

106

I went to the corner of my window seat and breathed in and out as Papa had shown me. It had been a while since I had done this. But after just a few minutes, I felt the knot in my stomach unwinding. I felt the anger abating and so I continued. When I opened my eyes, Sarah was looking at me.

"So, you have remembered that old lesson from Papa?"

"How did you know?"

"I have been doing the breathing as well. I have always done it; it helps me calm my nerves. It lets me be quiet inside as well as outside."

"Yes, I shall start again. Everyday. What do you say inside your head when you sit with the breathing, Sarah?"

"'Tis a secret," and with that she turned and walked away. I could see a half smile playing in that second before she turned. I thought, my little sister has a secret she is keeping from me, and I felt myself begin to laugh.

And then I wondered how could we smile or laugh in the midst of this grief and turmoil. How can we do that? Should we always be serious and sad and maybe angry? And I realized if we let ourselves be that way, we would do nothing. Then this Torquemada will surely be our victor because he will have stopped us from being who we are. We would give him the power to bring our lives to a halt. I understood better why my mother kept opening the door, and why Isaac had a new energy around the purpose of readying us for leaving. I had damped it down, pushed it under. I told myself I should not be finding any joy in this time of crisis and sadness. That being bereft I should be keening all the time. But I know that is not right. I do not want to forget the grief for my father, but I serve his memory better by seizing the challenge with all my strength and not being bowed down with loss.

So many things that father said to me over the years come back to me. And now they all fit into place, like a map with instructions. I realize they were not just philosophies, sayings and homilies that he shared. He was giving us directions to call upon, especially when things became difficult. It was a relief to know he was with me, with us, and that I could call up memory to guide me. I still wish I had his shoulder to lean on, the heft of him near me, but I can recall with clarity his teaching. That had been done with care, year after year, his wisdom seeping into me. It was a help. And we would all need help in the days to come.

I wrote stories before I could make my letters properly. I drew pictures on the slate and went to the kitchen to find mother or to the library to find my papa and tell them the story before I would erase it and begin another. Sometimes, father would write the story down in his own beautiful hand. On my ninth birthday, he presented me with a little book he had made. It was a collection of my stories. I remember my fingertips tracing the title, Stories by Chava, and my face breaking into a wide grin. I tingled all over; a book of my words just like the books in Papa's library. Holding that book now, perched on the window seat on this gray afternoon, I want that feeling back again. Sarah and Mama were both taking the siesta. But I could never sleep in the middle of the day, even as a small child I just lay in bed daydreaming. Now I sit here reading through my own words.

The first story was written when I was five. A small rabbit knocked on the window in the kitchen. It was winter and she was hungry. She had made steps with little stones so she could reach. Maria came to the garden and gave her a carrot and told her not to come back again. The rabbit scampered away and then looked back and put the carrot down and waved. I saw it all.

What an earnest little girl I was, without much of a fanciful imagination. I think I wanted to use the word scampered, a word I had just learned and nothing more. The book fell open to another story from a few years later. At night, when I am asleep, the stars chase the moon across the sky. There is a race to see who will first reach the sun before he comes out from under the earth. All night they run as fast as they can, but it is the sun that always wins because it is light before they reach the other side.

That sounds like me, wondering at how the heavens worked. I had made myself wake up in the middle of the night to try and see how the sky changed. I begged papa to let me sleep outside. Mama said an immediate no. I explained to papa that I needed to study the stars and he had said that in summer, when the weather was warm, perhaps we could. But by summer I lost interest and spent my days, when I wasn't studying or doing chores, searching for fossils and Roman stones. When Papa asked me, I said I was looking for time.

I tucked the little book under the pillow on the window seat when I heard Mama call. I was surprised to find her lying in bed. "Chava, fetch a cloth for my head please I have a terrible headache." When I returned with the cloth soaked in herbs and placed it on her forehead, I sat on the bed and asked, "You are worried Mama?"

"Of course I am, of course. I am so worried it feels like a mortar and pestle banging in my head. I do not like any of this. And I miss your father so."

"You do not have to pretend to be strong with me. I am strong enough for myself. And do not doubt Sarah."

"I do not doubt either of you." Mama took my hand.

"There is no need for you to carry more than your share."

"Well except that I am the mother."

"But you have raised us well Mama; we are saddened and worried, but we will be all right." I turned the cloth that rested on her forehead.

"…Ever your father's daughter."

"Yours, too. Don't think I don't see how much you manage, how much you have always managed Mama."

"Thank you for that. Now maybe you'll always listen to what I ask?"

"I didn't say that." I smiled and offered to fetch some tea.

"Yes, that would be nice, I feel better already. Thank you."

On the way down to the kitchen I thought this is the first time I remember mother lying in repose. I thought she looked old. I never really thought of ages for my parents, but they were much older than any of our friends' parents. Father had seemed so strong and then he was dead. Now Mama looked so fallible lying there. It made childhood seem ever further away.

April 23, 1492

Toledo

Chava watched the light change the room. She felt her sister turn and then settle back into sleep. Chava rose, wrapping the shawl around her, and went to the window. The fog was rising off the Tagus though the sky was clear. The storks' nest caught the slant of sun at the top of the tower. They had returned as they did each year. She wondered if they noticed the aftermath of the fighting when they flew from Africa over Granada, if they saw a beautiful city in defeat. She wondered if their shadows crossed the pools of the Alhambra. She remembered the constant whisper of water when they had all accompanied her father to see the caliph and visit scholars.

But now the caliph was vanquished. And the Alhambra was abandoned by the gentle voices of the women who sat with them, who served them nougats of almonds and sesame pastes, who laughed kindly at her faulty Arabic and responded by teaching them songs.

She imagined her own home empty, the wind clanging a door left unbarred. Then realized the house would not be abandoned. It would be taken over. Another family would live here. They would nail a cross above the mantle place and a statue of the virgin at the entrance way.

If all of them left all that would remain would be the indent on the doorframe from the mezuzah that her mother's family had brought from Montpellier. It was very old; silver filigree worked with Hebrew letters packed away, now with a copy of one of Maimonides books, and a Haggadah from the set that had been made for her family. These were the things they would carry closest to them. Along with jewels and coins and that which could buy them purchase in a place. Chava dressed and went downstairs to continue working with the books and the manuscripts. When she came into the library her mother was already there.

"Mama, have you been working all night?"

"I couldn't sleep child and there is so much to do."

"But there is time yet."

"Time will go quickly."

"I know, that is why you need me to stay here with you, to help you."

"Chava, you are leaving with Isaac and Sarah. That is final."

Chava returned upstairs to gather the books she kept tucked into the niche by the window seat where she like to read. There she felt the small roll of parchment she had not forgotten but had placed outside her thoughts for so long. It was sent by a messenger after Daniel's family had left Toledo. She had never opened it but had kept it. She broke the seal now. In his looped handwriting across the page were the words from a song they both loved, A fountain of blessings is your remembrances. Always. Always.

He had drawn a stem of lavender for devotion and flower of chamomile for patience. She folded it carefully until it was small enough to fit in the old treasure box. She put it in the pocket of her apron and patted it thinking she would decide later whether to place it in the box to carry away with her or not. She carried the rest of the books and manuscripts downstairs to the library. She gave her mother a kiss on the cheek. Her mother, she forgave for everything. Daniel, she was not sure if she ever could.

Chapter Six

The Leaving

April 1492
Toledo

CHAVA

Just before we left mother gave me a quill cut from the feather of a black stork, one of the great birds that return each year to its nest. With it, she gave me a bottle of ink and a journal bound in red patterned silk and said, "Write down everything, so even the daughters you have not yet had will know what the leaving was like."

"But Mama, surely you will join us in Portugal before I have daughters?" I tried to make light of it for moment. She would not. "If it comes to it, I will go to mass and kneel then come home and offer my real prayers in the cellar. I will hold what truth I know under my tongue." When she saw my eyes widen she softened her voice, "But I am sure I will leave before that is ever a possibility." When I protested yet again that Sarah and I could pretend with her if it came to that she said, "No, you would have to pretend your whole life. There is a storm coming in tonight; I think it will be a big one. The day after tomorrow you will go."

"Just a little while longer Mama, until the blossoms fall." But I knew it was useless. What difference can a few weeks make when it is forever that I am leaving? I wrapped the quill in a piece of linen and the bottle of ink in a piece of brocade. I opened the small book and took in its scent of newly pressed paper. I ran my fingers over one thick page after another as I counted off the things I was leaving: my feather bed, my new gown, the sun coming through the heavy-paned window in late afternoon, the sweet rising scent of challah from the bakery early Friday mornings, my great grandmother's silver candlesticks, my mother, my father's gravesite still without a marker, the stone I would never place there.

And so it began. We chose carefully what we would carry with us, gold sewn into seams, jewels pinned onto undergarments. This is what can be traded for a life. Mama knew these things; Papa had been an advisor to the royal court for many years and made sure she knew. "We are honored now," he had said, "but always there are whisperings about the Jews, and then violence breaks out. Torquemada so believes in his righteousness that he will sway the queen. "Keep this." He would say to Mama and he would hand her a piece of gold he had received from the king. My mother kept the coins and the gold chains and the ruby pendant and she gave it all to us. "Don't, Mama." I started to cry when she slipped off her heavy gold wedding band.

"Daughter, what does it matter? Here, see the mark on my finger? It shall remain until my skin dissolves away. This gold band might keep you safe for a month." And she smiled, how could she do that? I wept and she smiled. "It is already gone," she said.

ESTHER

I watch them leave. I feel the weight sewn into the seams of their garments. Even after they turn the corner, I feel the pull of my children. Glimpses of them as babies, as toddlers, as long-limbed girls, seemed to follow them through the arch like strands of embroidery threads unraveling. It broke my heart. As much as I knew there was no other way, it left me bereft.

My husband's voice was next to me. In the months since his death I heard it often. He would stay with me, but my daughters were gone. I pushed them to leave, wanting to save them from the flames, those lit or those that would burn from within, if they lived lies of their lives.

Afterwards, I went into the hall and Maria looked at me with her fig brown eyes. She had been with our family since I married. I know she understood what this cost me. Her sons had died in the holy wars. My daughters gone for no less a cause. She and I would keep each other's council. We both closed our hearts to the court of Spain, although I would still need to pretend in order to ensure the safe passage of my children and to carry out the plan to save all our legacies.

I expect Isaac's mother will be here shortly. She will lose her last remaining son. Such sadness, all brought on by the will of that mad man and the fears of the church. This has all happened before; it will happen again. How many times I wonder, how many more times?

CHAVA

I rode Leila through the gate and along the outside wall just ahead of Isaac on his chestnut and Sarah on her palfrey. We would meet further on with Jose and Juan who were bringing the mules bearing our luggage. The manuscripts were wrapped in cloths within clothes; coins and jewels were dispersed between them. The hope was that if some were found others would not be. A few of the rarer manuscripts were in each of the saddle bags as well.

The trip from Toledo to Salamanca could be made in five days, but with the mules and the wet roads it would likely take ten. There would be stops to visit family and friends, and to bring letters and plans from family to family. We paused at the curve to look back at the walls of the city in the thin light of an early, spring morning. The fog was rising up from the river making it look like a woman cloaked with a silken scarf.

Sarah rode up next to me and leaned over to pull my hood up, "We will need to take care of each other."

"I know.' I acknowledged.

"Yes, but will you let me?"

It was my turn to laugh, "Yes sister, I need you with me. I am so worried by leaving Mama behind. I think I hear our father telling me not to go."

"Listen to me big sister, I hear him saying we are doing just as we should. Besides sitting Shiva for him, this is the hardest thing I have ever done."

"For me as well sister. I hate this. Leaving all of this, leaving her."

"You could no more make our mother do what she does not want to do than you could make father. Really, I think she may have been the more determined of the two. Although sister, sometimes I think you surpass them both."

"No, the proof is we are here and she is not. You are right you know. I could bend Papa to at least think about changing his mind but with Mama there was no bending to be done."

"She believes this is the best choice, we must trust her." Sarah said firmly.

"Still, I am uneasy."

Isaac had gone back to meet Juan and Jose. I could see them approaching out of the gate onto the road. How small they looked against the great walls of Toledo, the Cathedral reaching into the sky at the top of the hill. It looked like a fortress. Cathedrals were built to be imposing, to reach as high toward their heaven as possible. Their own synagogue was subdued from without, nestled into the street. Inside the intricate stone, the wood carvings and inlays made it a place of quiet beauty. A place where words could be clearly heard and contemplated. Even though the holy of holy lay clothed in its own arc within the temple and the days of awe at the New Year and Yom Kippur demanded many hours at prayer in the synagogue the truest holy day came every week with the lighting of the Shabbat candles on Friday. Those were the most sacred moments, inside one's home; the daily rituals done without pomp or splendor. From the time we were very small we knew actions were more important than prayer. Papa used to say, "Your deeds are your prayers."

"Look," Sarah grasped my arm, "look up at the spire!" We watched as a black stork circled and then landed on its nest. It returned each year to the same place.

"Do you think we will return?" Sarah asked me.

"Maybe we will turn into storks."

We heard the voices of the others approaching then and took another look at the city, then turned our horses. We kept to a walk on the old Roman road leading north and east into the first day of our journey away from home.

ESTHER

I listened for a long time to the receding clip-clop of their horses' hooves. I let my head fill with anything but the picture of them riding further and further away. I thought of Benjamin arguing with his colleagues Ali and Jose Maria. Oh, how they all relished those discussions. At the end they would say, "Well, after all, there is one god at each of our beginnings." They would begin and end with that same phrase. In between were all the differences. Now, that conversation would be unimaginable. The upcoming journey of Colon will have cousins of mine on his ships, disguised as I may one day be disguised.

We were taught that differences are good things, that it makes us sharper, keeps our arguments stronger, lets us recognize the shape and curve of things, but now the king and queen are wanting one Spain, one unified Spain where everyone believes in a trinity under the holy church.

There are times I think, what is the difference if there is holiness in everything, as Maimonides wrote. If everything holds the breath of god, the imprint of angels on each of us, what difference can a name make? But when a man like Torquemada says there is only one way of thinking, well then you must make the other ways disappear. I don't know whether to be more afraid of staying or more scared of leaving, more worried about changing or never being able to change.

CHAVA

We stop for a brief rest at Rieves. I dismount and my foot hits a patch of dry dirt scattering dust like a spill of stars. It looks like magic. Is there such a thing as an ordinary miracle? The way thread fits in the eye of the needle in the steadiness of my sister's hand. The way she stitches together what had come asunder. The way Maria chops what she's brought in from the ground- onions, carrots, turnips, and the rough tops of the leaves, then fries, in oil, then stirs. She turns it into stew which we eat with yesterday's bread warmed in the oven, spattered with water and salt so it tastes new again. The way the letters in books transform into the alleys of Marrakesh and the towers of London, the walls of water on the great Indian sea and rivulets in a desert oasis. I have never left Spain but have journeyed in time and space, tracing the shape of alphabets that come from other places. Languages that once rolled in the mouths of people who have now become dust. How is it that the past makes its way into today?

And the weight of light, how the sun comes through the glass of the library windows and makes the ink lift off the page. I am going to keep a list of miracles like this. Not the grand stories in the Torah or Koran, not the battles of the Upanishads or the wars of the Greeks, but these daily miracles: the color of morning, the merging of calls from the minaret, the cathedral bells, and the stork gliding back to its nest again this year.

The morning was drizzly, but the afternoon opened with enough sun to warm. The rains stayed at bay as the land rose and dipped and rose again toward Torrijos. It was a town of passing. A place to rest that first night. We went to the home of family acquaintances. We had stayed with them before on the first day of other journeys with mother and father. It was strange to arrive at the house and be greeted by the señora who as she kissed each of us on both cheeks shook her head in between. "And your mother?", she asked. I took her hands and said she will be coming soon. I wanted to believe that, and that belief must have resonated in my voice. She smiled back at me.

Juan and Jose made sure the animals were seen to before they took their meal in the kitchen. We sat in the dining room where some obvious care had been taken. We made conversation as well as we could. Thank goodness our tiredness was noticed as both our hosts waved us early to bed saying we would need an early start the next day. The three of us would sleep inside the house; there was a bed for Sarah and me to share. Isaac would have a pallet in the kitchen. "You will be the warmest", we teased. I wrote in the journal by candlelight at the little table in the room we shared.

We were gone early from Torrijos thanking our hosts for their hospitality and for the food they packed for us. They pointed out that they were giving us bread and cheese. Sparing us from having to refuse their fine jamon. Toledo lay behind, beyond our realm of sight. We were gone. We passed the Castillo de la vela at Maqueda which held no invitation for us and started to climb more as we continued toward Almorox. The walls of Toledo were replaced by the walls of the Sierra de Gredos stretching across the horizon in front of us.

The Sierra was cloud covered and the road only a gentle climb at first. We went at an easy pace letting the horses and ourselves become used to the movement. As we rode through the day the weather held. There was enough of a breeze from the mountains that I kept my extra shawl around me. The River Tajo was long gone, the hills of home now just a haze behind us. The mountains in front of us becoming taller and taller.

The lands grew drier as we rose into the foothills. There were olive and fig trees and pines. We passed pastures and wheat fields. As we came to the Guadarrama there were clusters of low trees. We passed small houses close together where the families who tend the fields lived. And still we climbed. Before we reached Almorox we gave the horses their own rein, letting them run through field that beckoned speed. At the edge we stopped for them to drink and straightened our own appearances. We checked our packs and loads and came slowly in to the pueblo. Two beautiful horses-one white, one black- were pastured by one of the first dwellings. Almorox was a long town following the curve of hill. We would stay in the home of the winemakers there. We had sent a message the day before letting them know we would arrive before sunset. We passed the vineyards and saw the large house at the curve of the hill. We had never stayed here before, but they were cousins of cousins. We knew we would be welcomed.

Chapter Seven

The Journey

Toledo to Avila

Chava's Journal

There is little that appears soft in Toledo, so much is made of rock and stone. Only the light and the reach of sky seem like they might give way. We left in the late morning passing through the la Puerta del Cambron. The arch leading us out of Toledo from the Juderia. We paused there within its deep shadows. I looked back on the narrow streets toward home and then turned and looked toward the northwest. Our path would lead us away from Toledo's hills and toward the mountains. I could not imagine much beyond that.

We stood under the stone of the arch that had been there for centuries before us and likely would remain long after every one of us was gone. Juan and Jose had gone ahead with the mules. We had not yet mounted our horses. I wanted the stone under my own feet still. Isaac tipped his head back and took in a deep breath. He let out the first note of the Shema. The prayer echoed and filled us. We turned away from our home, mounted, and let the clatter of our horses' hooves fill the descent toward the fields.

I remember the moment on that first day when we looked back on the hills of Toledo, a rolling bank of fog behind the city spires and in front of us the Sierra de Gredos began to claim its shape. The rising mountains looked like clouds when we first left the city and now we are rising up into them. This is all the heaven I am likely to see.

April 27, 1492

The reins were smooth and warm in Chava's bare hands as they rested their horses in the shade of a chestnut tree. The water still held the coolness of early morning, when they had filled their skins before leaving Don Manuel's in Almorox. Today they would ride through the afternoon so they could reach the Fernandez villa near Tiemblo de Avila before dark. Don Manuel had advised against them stopping in the pueblo of San Martin, "Better to keep to the road", he said. He had taken Isaac aside then and spoken to him with a look of consternation. Chava trusted Isaac would tell them what was said once they were away, and as soon as they rode off Isaac did.

"He told me that these were dangerous times and not to trust easily."

"Really, that was all? It seemed to take a much longer time."

"I was getting to that. He asked that I deliver a message to Señor Zacuto in Salamanca."

"And can you not tell us?" Sarah asked.

"I will if you stop interrupting." He looked from one to the other. "He said, Señor Zacuto would do well to leave sooner rather than later. Another cousin was told that his name had come up in conversation between Torquemada and the queen."

"But why?" Chava asked.

"It seems that there are lists being made and tallies being taken of who is worth what. Señor Zacuto has much knowledge that could be used to further exploration. There is concern that if he leaves, he will share that with another kingdom."

"And other names Isaac, do you know of other families that are being talked about?"

"Your father's, of course, but the queen quickly said may he rest in peace. There was nothing said of your mother. I asked."

"And can no message be sent to the Zacutos' to warn them?"

"It has been done, but we were asked to emphasize the importance of leaving now. He thought us wise to be on our way."

"Let us do that then." Sarah said as she turned her horse back toward the road. There was nothing more to be said. Each of them was thinking of those they had left behind. They had permission to leave Spain but knew that the eyes of the coming Inquisition were already turned on them, watching the contacts between families, observing who was going where. Who sheltered who might reveal the true converts from the Judaizers that sullied the church. Torquemada was a man set on vengeance; few fell beyond his suspicion. Thanks to her father's connections they could make it all the way to Portugal staying in the homes of trusted families.

After the massacres in Sevilla many families outwardly converted. They relinquished their beloved Andalusia as their father's family had and moved into Christian Spain. Those that remained outwardly Jewish did not come under the scrutiny of the Inquisition, but the hatred of it was still felt. The New Christians, the Anusim as those forced to convert were called, were often doubted by the Old Christians. They went to mass on Sundays but continued to practice the customs they had always observed. Only now they did so in secret.

There were a number of families who had kept their status and remained openly Jewish as theirs had done. When she asked her father why families became Conversos, he shook his head. "Daughter there are those who are meant to do one thing and those who are meant to do another. Judgment is not for us to hold. We all make our ways the best we can through the world. Each of us is given a different road to travel."

But Chava knew the casting down of his eyes meant he was thinking far more than he said. Now that her mother had chosen to stay behind and was even entertaining the possibility of at least appearing to consider converting, who was she to condone or condemn? Still, there was some pride in keeping their traditions openly.

Both of them knew many families who lived one life outside in the world and another inside in their homes. They hid a mezuzah in the foot of the Madonna they kept at the entry way and kissed it on the way in and way out. Her family kept their mezuzah in plain sight on their doorway and her father's close status with the king kept anyone from scorning them. Though she knew there were whispers, she could feel them like small currents of air following her through the market or down the street on Friday nights when they came from temple. But it was like bees buzzing past her, they didn't sting, just kept her wary.

When she told her father of the feeling, he said wariness was never a bad thing. Wary and watchful were good, especially in these times. It was fear that was to be guarded against because fear made you do stupid things. Wariness kept you smart. They were taught the difference and learned it well. Sarah did not go about as much as Chava did. Sarah was content to be at home where Chava had always been pulled to the edges of things, the end of the street that looked out to the fields, the top of the hill. She begged her father often to let her go with him to court or on visits; and he often indulged her.

The grief of his loss was a weight she felt daily. She kept a note he had written her the week before he died folded tight into a small, silk purse she wore about her neck. It was just a note like many others that he wrote before he set out on a visit. But this was the last one in his hand.

Loss upon loss. Chava wondered if he had lived and had gone with Abravenel and Seneor to the king, might his voice have been the one to sway the royals away from Torquemada's insistence on the edict? But there was no good in thinking what could never be. It was better to think what could be. For now, it was best to watch the road, to look ahead and not behind.

April 28, 1492

The smell of damp wool clung all around them. It was the fourth day of traveling and whatever buoyancy they had felt during the first few days had disappeared in the unforgiving rain. There was nothing for it but to pull their heads back inside the hoods of their cloaks and ride on. They moved at a slow pace. The roads were muddy. It had been raining since yesterday and their progress was slowed by slippery roads and the dank wet weather. They decided to stop at the house of the brothers Diaz. Cousins of cousins of Isaac's, they had left the city a generation ago to take up a large swath of land where they raised bulls and wheat. Chava and Sarah had met them only once when they came to Toledo during Succoth and their family had come to pass the evening in the open dwelling erected for each harvest celebration. Every Jewish family built one and each was a different style but always you could see the stars through the woven branches. And always there was laughter and stories inside. It was a happy holiday.

As they paused, they shared out some of the bread left over from their breakfast. It was hard, but it filled them up well enough. Chava wondered if she would ever be dry again. For a moment the sun broke through and steam rose from their cloaks and then the sun went again behind the cloud and a drizzle started up. Well, at least it was not pouring as it had been earlier. Chava thought of all the times she envied the travelers out on their way, along the road, wishing now for her own chair in the library by the fire. Thinking of her mother alone in the house was too troubling though. She felt herself shiver and said to the others, "Come now, let us ride on. We are going so slowly, we can pass food back and forth between us as we ride, but at least we will be getting ourselves closer."

"She's right, as she most always is." Isaac tried a laugh. He was working hard to keep up their spirits. There were so many more days yet to go, and at the rate they seemed to be moving even more than the days they had originally thought. One of the mules had thrown a shoe yesterday which caused delay. They were a day behind and the rain showed no sign of stopping.

"Let us just get there. I keep seeing my feet by a fire and I want the rest of me to feel the warmth." Sarah tried to keep her voice light, but the heaviness came through. They rode along narrow roadways wide enough only for a small cart. They could see vineyards on the rise to either side of the road; most kept their wheat closest to the road to protect the grapes from being picked at by those passing by. The same was true for fruit trees or any planting that would yield itself for easy taking. Though there was nothing growing yet. The last time that the girls had passed this way had been in late August when the fields were high and the harvest ready for taking. Now at the beginning of spring, the planting had just begun.

Sarah rode next to her sister, the horses at a steady walk now in the lighter rain. "It is strange to think we will not taste any of what is being planted. I put in the early herbs for mother before we left. I hope Maria remembers to care for them."

"I am sure she will, sister. I was thinking of last year's Succoth. Of how we built it so it was ready when Papa returned from his trip, remembering the songs we sang, the way the new wine tasted."

" I want to only think of a good warm meal and being off my horse for the rest of the day."

"We have a ways to go yet, but we are closer. Two more hours, at most, I would think."

"Can we not pick up the pace just a little?"

Chava glanced at her sister with the beginnings of grin. She clicked at her horse and moved into a fast walk. Sarah kept right next to her and they realized within a few minutes everyone had sped up just a bit. They went a bit faster still. They did not dare for a trot, at the risk of one of the mules slip-sliding, but at least they would be there just a bit sooner.

They arrived at the finca in the Valle de Iruelos before dark. The air was full of pine and wet wood and the rain tasted of granite. Juan had ridden ahead to let the brothers know they had been riding since morning and had not stopped to eat. When they came into the courtyard they were greeted, and their horses taken from them. The men unloaded the mules and put the trunks safely in the large entry way and their cloaks were hung to dry. They were escorted to a fire and given mulled wine. Already the damp was leaving them and the wine warming them.

April 29, 1492

The brothers had many questions for them, but they had fewer answers. Isolated as they were they had little news, only rumors of the edict had reached them. Their family had never converted but, as there was no temple or community of other Jews nearby, they kept to their own ways, observing the Sabbath and the holidays quietly. They went to bed early and had a good breakfast of boiled eggs, cheese and bread. Even though they were well-rested and well fed, they left heavyhearted. Perhaps it was the mountains looming in front of them and the clouded morning that let no light through. There were few signs of spring here at all.

Chava felt the weight of each step press into the ground as they rode. She did not know a day could consist of so many steps and yet could feel still as if you were no closer to the place you were trying to reach. All of them had traveled distances even longer than this, but somehow this felt to be slower and heavier than any other trip. It was laden with the burden of being gone without the promise of return. They had turned from children into adults and that made the progress weighted and long.

Chava imagined a map of steps unwinding like a spiral stair, taking her away from what she had known. Not just her city but her home where she had been a daughter, all that was being cast away with each step. She left the path of her own proscribed future behind as they rode further from Toledo's walls. She thought of the silversmith's shop and the little pendant she had been hoping for. She thought of the marzipans they ate, especially at Passover, shaped into the story of exodus. The last of the sweets brought away with them, eaten just the day before.

The twisting, turning streets always going up and down and the river almost circling around. The gates into the city and the bakers and the vintner's shops, all of that not to be seen again. She thought she had said goodbye but now as she rode with each back and forth, with each rocking plodding step, she felt like she was saying goodbye again and again to them. And goodbye to that girl she was. She wondered who would reappear on the other side of the Duero after they crossed into Portugal? Who would that Chava be? Would she be any different than the one who lived in Toledo? Who would she be without the window seat and the street below, without her father and now without her mother? Her thoughts went round and round, even as the line they rode was straight between the towns and the sun made its arc across the sky.

She heard her name like an echo and was brought up short from her musings as she realized Isaac was signaling for a stop. Drawing up under a wide ash tree to rest the horses and dismount to eat and drink. She shook herself and swung her leg over and slid down. Leaning a moment into her horse, she felt Leila's warmth and the strong arch of her neck and wondered if this could be enough, just this, a day without rain, her horse and her beloved sister. After a short while they rode on into the snow-peaked Sierra de Gredos. They could feel the winds coming down from the mountains, bringing the cold, as they continued toward Salamanca.

They were heading west even though there was a pull east. Not just the old stories of Jerusalem, but the recent invitation from the Ottoman empire. Her mother was sure though it was best to go to Portugal first. With proximity to the sea future routes could be more easily decided. Her mother warned them against the easy temptation to go south toward the Mediterranean or east toward Cataluña and Barcelona. She thought the passages that way would become costlier and more dangerous. More people would flee in the old directions.

Chava was not sure if somehow it was not the conversations with Colon, or the maps he had shown her mother and father the previous Autumn. He had been their guest at the bidding of Louis Santangel and shown them the voyage he had been planning for so long.

Her father had met him some years before and thought Colon to be a man who might hold a secret. She had watched them once in her father's study, their heads bowed over an old Hebrew text. Colon asking her father to translate, saying he could only read some of the words. He apologized for his lack of schooling. But her father thought he had a ray of brilliance about him. He was not afraid to think differently, and he sought counsel from Moors and Jews, though he was a professed Christian. Certainly, her father, and most of the men with whom he kept council, believed the earth was round and circled its way around the sun. These were men who spoke with scientists and considered learning to be a part of faith and not an attack on it, as so many of their Christian neighbors did.

There was the dividing line between Christians, Muslims and Jews about truth being enlightening, even if it challenged the doctrines of faith. Faith was stronger than a set of facts; faith was what carried you to pursue truth. Truth neither upheld faith, nor diminished it. It was why the arguments between Jews and Christians ended with a winner and a loser and why the arguments between Muslims and Jews led to more discoveries.

But that was from the time of the Golden Age, when argument was still considered worthy. Now with the influence of Torquemada, and those like him, it was thought best to send whoever disagreed away.

CHAVA

Sarah sliced the dried apricots and then mixed them with the dry pitted cherries and almonds. I portioned these out with bread and cheese so as not have to stop for food along the way. We needed to make better time today. It was Friday and we wanted to arrive well before sundown to another of Isaac's cousins' home. Neither Sarah nor I had ever met them before. They converted long ago in the large wave that came after the uprisings of 1391. The same riots that had driven father's family from Al Andalus to Toledo. We stopped at a creek to let the horses drink. We had ridden well all morning.

I heard Sarah asking Isaac, "But if they are Conversos, why is it so important to them that we arrive well before sundown?"

"Sarah, they are Anusim, not willing Conversos. You know the difference. It was the threat of death to their children that forced them to pretend to convert."

"They keep the Sabbath?" I asked.

"Yes, they do, and Passover and the high holy days as well. They do the best they can; but to all their neighbors and especially to the lords that are close by, they are known as good Christians."

"So, it is possible then, to keep your faith intact and live like you belong to the rest of Spain?" I looked pointedly at Sarah.

"It is possible, but it takes a great toll. And it will only become more and more difficult from now on. We know those who play the part. Look at your Daniel." Sarah grabbed Isaac's arm. Daniel's name was not a topic of conversation I welcomed.

I took a deep breath to control my anger. "He is no longer my Daniel, remember that Isaac. The relationship ended when his family chose conversion. I don't think they are Anusim. I think they are Marranos." I could not help but spit out the insult.

"Chava," her sister gripped her arm, "you sound like one of them. And do not think that we could do this, our family is too well known. Mama is right. Stop thinking you can change that."

Isaac looked from me to Sarah, "What are you talking about?"

Sarah replied with a hard glance at Chava, "She keeps thinking we could have stayed behind and pretended conversion. The decision has been made."

"Chava how can you curse at Daniel and his family and yet be wanting to do the same thing?"

"It is not the same, not the same at all. They had a choice, he had a choice and he chose the easier road."

"What makes you think it was an easy road? Chava, sometimes I do not understand you." Isaac had been close with Daniel; they had studied and played together. Sarah took her sister's hand to try and calm her.

"His family chose to convert so that they could advance more easily. We were not looking to make our lives easier. We are trying to save the books; it would be pretense, nothing more."

"And what makes you so certain they had a choice Chava?" Isaac looked at her hard, "You may not know all you think you know."

Sarah put her other hand to Isaac's shoulder and said, "We must go. Juan and Jose are waiting ahead for us. The sun is moving more quickly than we are." As Isaac mounted, Sarah drew Chava close to her and whispered, "We will talk more of this later." Her sister squeezed her hand, but Sarah saw her bite her lip. Chava considered what it would be like to always have to keep a constant check on one's every action. Not so much different from what I must do most of the time, she thought. But then maybe, maybe, that was not quite true.

April 30, 1492

They arrived at the house an hour before the sun went down. The evening light caught the dust on the curtains and the glass vases. It lent an eeriness to the old room. The room was at the very top of the stairs in a part of the house that was no longer used. The serving boy had brought up two pallets of hay and when Chava turned to ask where Isaac would sleep, the boy said the mistress of the house had put him in the cellar. It would be warm enough at this time of year and she had placed a good thick pallet for him down there.

Sarah thanked the young boy and asked him to be sure their groomsmen would have a place to sleep, and the horses be well cared for. Of course Senorita, he answered, as he backed out of the room. Sarah almost giggled, backing out of the room like that was for lords and ladies and certainly they were not that.

"I would love a wash, wouldn't you?" Chava said, as she took off her gloves and removed the scarf she had around her head.

"Hot rose water," Sarah answered, "and the lavender soap that Maria makes."

"Well I would settle for not cold and dried grass to rub my skin with."

A young woman knocked on the still open door just then. And in answer to their hopes, she said the Senora of the house was filling a tub for them in the kitchen below and would cordon off the room from any of the men if they would like to bathe before the Sabbath began.

"Tell her we are most grateful." The girl curtsied and Sarah and Chava grasped each other's hands and twirled around as they had as small girls.

I guess they are truly Anusim," Sarah said, "washing before the Sabbath."

"We will be clean and warm tonight. And I dare say have a good meal. It was a long day was it not, sister?"

"Each day, we are further from home, seems longer." Sarah said, a break in her voice.

"Each day we are closer to Aunt and Uncle's and getting the books to safety." Sarah tried a small smile. Contentment was a fleeting thing.

They took off their outer layers and went down the back stairs to the kitchen as the young girl instructed them. The kitchen was warmed with the fires stoked and a large steaming tub in the middle of the room with a scent of almonds.

The matron smiled at them, "Ah, you girls look like you can use a little warmth." At that Chava almost began to cry in that bittersweet way tears rising, throat closing not for sadness or any apparent reason. But then kindness was no small thing. And the tub was big enough for them both. After they had dried and dressed, they were asked to follow the señora down to the cellar. It was not at all what they imagined. There, below ground, was a table set with a beautiful cloth and a tureen of steaming soup. There were candles set in silver candlesticks and a goblet set for wine. And a challah, braided and perfectly golden. Her husband had changed into clean clothes. She placed a scarf over her head and said the prayer, just the way they did at home. She smiled at them when she finished and offered the blessing for children to all three of them. They bowed their heads gratefully.

They stayed through the Sabbath. On Saturday morning there were prayers and then the rest of the day was spent reading and talking, much as it would have been at home. For dinner there was stew, cholent, cooked since the afternoon before so that no work would need to be done on the Sabbath. It was so much like home- chickpeas with greens and chicken and lamb, challah from the night before. At dark, everyone helped with chores and woke early on Sunday morning. After they thanked their hosts for the respite, they left with the hopes of arriving to Avila by evening.

CHAVA

It was the first time I felt at home since we had left. I hugged Isaac's cousin, Ducela, goodbye. She said to me as she held both my hands, "Child, life is not so difficult as you might think. We have the mountains; we have fields; we have the grace of g-d above us and below and we know who we are. No matter what others think, we know." Her words stayed with me as I rode. She had given me much to consider.

Papa traveled often. He had been at least five times to the North of Africa visiting Fez, Tunisia and Tetuan. More times even to Granada, and of course to the Arribes as well as Porto and Lisboa. He had even been once to London and at least twice to Amsterdam. But the longest journey by far had been to the great city we still called Constantinople. He went there on behalf of the king. The company on that journey were two of each, as the king said, two Jews, two Muslims and two Christians, all learned men. But this was before the king had begun to be swayed against us. And though Papa had kept his position at court and never completely lost his access to the king, he knew that our influence was waning by the summer of 1491.

Little did we know then that it would be all of our families last high holy days in Spain, the last celebration of harvest we would ever have together.

I remember that when Papa left for Constantinople, I begged him to bring me back an elephant. "Ah daughter, the elephants live even further away. I am not going all the way to the India. Just to Turkey, my dear. But perhaps an elephant will be lost there, after the spices have been brought."

"Oh please, papa, find one. A baby will do just fine."

"You are wise, daughter, to want something that can carry you, but I will bring you back something I can carry instead. Always best the small things you can put in a pocket or in the fold of a cape. Always best not to rely on someone else to carry you."

He brought me back a tiny elephant carved from turquoise and bearing a small nugget of gold and one of silver. "Here my love," he said when he returned, "here is your pachyderm." I had half expected to see him return leading a beast like the pictures I had seen in the manuscripts he shared with us. I swallowed my disappointment quickly. Even at five I knew how to take what was offered and then store my own dreams away to be brought out later. It is not that I ever gave up on wanting that elephant, I just imagined the figurine into a real one and let myself wander on its back, across the plains of La Mancha, all the way to the Mediterranean.

He was gone nearly six months on that trip and mama asked him if he could not leave for so long again. I miss you too much Benjamin, she said, it is too long and who knows… She would drift off then, remembering something that I did not yet know about. That look of hers came to me only after I had left, only after I understood that longing was not something that came from what you never had, what you never knew, but only from what you had once had and would never have again. That was the look in my mother's eyes when we left, and it was the look I remember from my childhood when she would ask my Papa for something even he could not grant her. I did not understand then what was hidden in her words. That she longed to feel what she had not felt in so long; that she was safe; that she was home; that it would not be taken away again.

I carried the elephant with me when we left Toledo, it fit in the palm of my hand. I knew it was worth a great deal of money, but I promised myself I would not sell it unless it was the last thing left. I bargained with myself. I would sell the gold nugget and the silver, but not the poor little beast that had already traveled so far and had carried me though so many of the journeys I imagined as a child.

But amidst all this sadness there was a spark that I felt. A small edge of light that drove me to write in the journal, to ready my things, that made me, dare I admit it, excited to go. I had always dreamt of journeys to far off places like the ones Papa would carry stories home about from the court. I never wanted to leave forever, of course, but I did long to go. My sister, Sarah, had no desire to leave even our street. I remember overhearing Papa's voice once when he was talking to Isaac's father about me, "That one will burn herself on the candle so she can know." I was so proud when he said that. I held onto that memory and thought, "I will take that spark and use it. I will." I knew my Papa would want me to.

Chapter Eight

The Convent near Avila

CHAVA

By afternoon, the clouds rolled over the sun, darkening the sky. A sudden wind bore the cold of the Pyrenees. All at once, spring vanished. I wrapped my cloak tighter, realizing it would be prudent to stop for the night sooner than we had expected. There was a village just beyond the meseta. None of us had ever been there before. We knew some of the smaller towns had no kindness for strangers and less for Jews. We could only hope that a Jewish family, or at least a family of Conversos, lived there.

Until now, we had no need to explain why we were journeying beyond stating that we were on our way to visit family. But before entering the village, we decided to add that Isaac was returning to his studies in Salamanca and so he had offered to accompany us. It provided some prestige and more of a reason why we were together. Isaac could speak well enough about Salamanca. Sarah was closing her eyes in a quick prayer that we would not have to stay at an inn, when a gust brought down the first drops of rain. I called out to move faster. Jose and Juan would be able to catch up when we stopped.

Isaac knocked on the first door we came to and asked where we might find a place to sleep. He was told there was a convent close by that housed travelers. Isaac requested the villager let Jose and Juan know where we had gone. When he agreed, Isaac gave him a coin to bind him to his word. It started to rain in earnest just as we reached the walled convent. I dismounted first and knocked on the gate. A young novice came to the door and told us we were welcome to come in, but any men would have to stay in the stone barn in the outer courtyard. Isaac nodded at us to go on. The young woman promised she would send out food and blankets. In turn, I promised a donation to the convent. I tried not to give any indication of the weight sewn into my cloak and gown. The women here would know how to read Latin, so I was grateful that the manuscripts were packed safe away. If they saw them, they might well recognize the books and scrolls for what they were.

The novice took us through to meet the Mother Superior. Sarah grasped my hand. I had to remind myself that we were doing nothing wrong, at least not yet. We were still within the borders of Spain and could not be accused of anything. I squeezed Sarah's hand to reassure her.

The Mother Superior bade us sit in front of her desk. It was a large desk, scrolls sat in one corner, a leather bound ledger in another. In front of her, there was a quill that looked as if she had set it down in mid-sentence on top of a partially filled parchment. We sat in the two chairs in front of the desk facing her. The novice bowed and left us. The fire had been recently fed. By its light I saw that she looked somewhat older than my mother. I noticed her fingers had ink marks on them, always a sign to me of someone that might be trusted, someone who at least loved words well enough to leave the mark of them on her.

"Thank you, Madam, for giving us shelter for the night and for our cousin." I thought it best to claim Isaac as family.

"Is that who the young man is? I was only told he was quite handsome and had a regal bearing."

"He is our cousin on his way to Salamanca where he studies."

The woman had a glint of a laugh in her eyes, "And you are on your way to study as well?"

I laughed out right. Sarah gave me a warning glance. "It is quite all right." She smiled at Sarah and as she did so the lines in her face lightened. I could see the young woman she once had been.

"No madam," I answered, "though I wish I could."

"Here, as you can see," she held up her hands, "I am able to study. Do you read?"

"Yes, madam." I answered without wanting to give away too much.

"Then perhaps you could help an old woman with failing eyes." She took up the parchment closest to her and, unrolling it, handed it to me.

"Shall I read it out to you madam?" She nodded and folded her hands together on the desk. I leaned a bit to catch more light from the sconce on the wall. "I am writing you, my friend, to ask a favor. We know you have in your convent a library much greater than appearances would lead one to think. I hope you will consider adding to it. There are some tomes which I am afraid will not survive the rising scrutiny and I believe these works must be safeguarded. I think you will not come under the same scrutiny we will face here in the city. These are translations into Castilian done at the time of Alfonso the Wise. There are works from both the Hebrew and Arabic. I pray you will take them into your care."

I stopped then and looking up at her found her smile broad and bright, "And do you need me to write you an answer madam?" Sarah took in her breath at my audacity, but I felt safe. Something told me I was with another scholar, one who knew the honor of study and translation, who understood carrying knowledge from one people to another was vital and worthy.

"I have already replied," She looked down toward the letter in front of her. My eyebrows raised into a question before I could stop myself. She smiled back at me," I said yes, I would be delighted. I thought you might be the messenger."

"No, we are not messengers."

"Yes, of course," she said, "you are on your way to Salamanca. But you will take some supper with me and look at a manuscript for me with your sharp eyes?" Sarah still looked uneasy, but the woman rose and said, "You are safe here, daughters. We are of the older houses. You are safe with us."

We stayed for two nights while the storm rose. I woke in the middle of the night hearing a soft chanting. For a moment, I thought I was home. Then, I recognized what I heard. The nuns reciting the liturgy in Latin. I tried to go back to sleep but could not. My own litany filled my head. I thought of all those things I would never see again. The field in fall after the harvest. The field that belonged to our family but tended by Maria's. Her family and mine have been entwined for decades as it had always been on the peninsula. Christians and Jews, Muslins and Jews, our three peoples braided like the harvest garlic we all used in our cooking.

Perhaps, that is what made me think of that harvest time. One year, I believe I was nine and Sarah was seven, we decided to build our sukkah in the field under the wide expanses of stars. We were always so glad for Sukkot coming, just days after the solemnness of Yom Kippur, and that year had been an especially good harvest. Usually we built the hut right in our own courtyard, but it was so mild Father thought it would be good for all of us to spend the night where you could clearly see the wide expanse of heaven. We gathered sheaths and vines, branches that the tree had cast off, leaves and late blooming flowers, stalks of sunflowers. Papa and Isaac's father built the frame. All the children from the farming families helped to

142

decorate the sukkah. We worked with them to assure we left space to see the sky. We set a cooking fire outside and they slaughtered a goat and some chickens. We roasted the meat all afternoon.

That evening we sat all together and feasted. We watched the stars come out and counted the ways to walk through the heavens. We sang songs and the children drifted off to sleep together under that one large sky, resting on G-d's good ground, and in everything that feeds us.

Someday I will go there again. I know it will not be that sukkah, or even that field, but I will return to a sense of home. A place that is mine. Or, if it is not mine, then to a place that harbors me. One that shelters us, allowing us to grow a community there. Surely there will be someplace like that where the sky will stretch past what we know and I can fall asleep again under the stars, under the night before it has turned cold. I fell back to sleep, my sister's breathing a comfort, as it had always been, the chanting of the nuns a soft wind.

On the second day the Mother Superior welcomed Isaac into her office and showed us some of the old manuscripts she kept. I think she had an idea of who we were and what we carried with us. At the end of our visit she showed me one of the old books on the shelf behind her, as far from the fire and smoke as it could be. "This was a translation done by Abelard himself. We have kept things safe before; we will do so again."

"The Abelard who put learning as the highest rule of law?" I could barely contain my excitement as she placed the manuscript on the table before me.

There was a question in her voice that I took to be an invitation. We spoke then about the school of translators. How countries are not just physically bound lands but ways of thinking and perceiving the world. How languages can be borders or bridges. Borders that allowed meaning to seep through and where people could see the other side. In every tongue people speak- of loved ones, of land, of work and food, of warmth and shelter and home, of fear, of G-d, of weather.

When she asked about Toledo, I said it was a city made of countries. Spain is a country made of nations. I can barely imagine what lies beyond. Swirling colors and words in different languages that rise together into a widening sky. And while I was comfortable with her, I was not so trusting as to reveal what we carried. There was a part of me that wanted to stay with her for weeks, reading and discussing the way I used to do with Papa. I never doubted that she understood knowledge might be as sacred as prayer.

As we went to sleep, I thought again about that sukkah. I felt so safe in that open place. The sky came through and my parents' voices drifted in and out of my sleep; there was a thank you on our lips. Gratitude for the harvest coming in and a place to store it and rejoice in it. Perhaps that is home then, the place that feels safe. Somewhere where the sky meets the land and you can sleep with voices all round you that are filled with grace.

Tomorrow we'll ride across more fields readying for planting. Some just being turned, some still waiting for the plough, some vineyards where the very earliest of the leaves are tinging to green. I conjure images in my mind's eye as we move ever further away from my own home. In Spain there are always mountains to be crossed. Five sierras rise on the peninsula. Father always had us study the maps and memorize the names of places. He would describe villages to us with uncanny detail. In the blacksmith's shop it was so hot everyone's face turned red inside the shed where the burly man worked in a glow; the village where the baker's small empanadas filled with sheep cheese would always make a ready lunch. La Alberca, where the women sold turron and obleas on the street. The mountains became, to us, a series of villages and the villages streets filled with people. The map no longer appeared as lines and obstacles, demarcations and bounded land, but full of stories and voices and languages.

Languages change as you journey from one place to another, but it was not just the words strung together that shifted. It was what they described. And the way they lilted across a phrase, the weight of the phrase itself. As translators we knew to look for these clues so when we moved from one language to another it was with more than words. It was with implications and suggestions. In one language a bird's flight could mean escape, avoidance; in another, it could be lifted on wings of love. How to keep the intent with threads and lines that remain invisible to all but other translators?

There are moments I think that converting is just a matter of kneeling and reciting the prayers I have heard seep from the church doors. What could be easier than that? Professing words, like reciting a poem. But then, as if someone was to pull back a tapestry on a room, I see that it is my whole life I would need to change. The rhythm of my days, the food I eat, the songs we sing when we are working in the garden. And even more the way I think. I have been taught to ask questions. Questions frame my thoughts. But the Christians do not ask so many questions. They learn what to believe and then they believe it, or so it seems to me. Of course, there are exceptions, like the Mother Superior. But they do not have text along the margins of their books, question upon question, debate upon debate like we do. The only debate I have heard them engage in are the arguments between us and them, an argument of right or wrong without nuance. I realize I could not pass as a Converso. What would my day be like without questioning? It seems impossible to be someone who bows her head and accepts the words of others.

Chapter Nine

The Journey

Avila to Salamanca

Chava's journal

We left just before the planting, as if we were the seeds scattered, after the early spring storms, when the days were clear, but not too cold. We tried to understand why we had moved from the periphery of their lives to the center of their hatred. Why our neighbors had become our enemies? In the first days of journeying westward towards Portugal, I wrote about the towns we passed through; what we ate, where we slept, but then it became so hard, and the days began to drift one into the other.

Sometimes I forget why I am writing but then I remember my mother's voice and so I write. I take my quill and dip it in the ink and give a voice to the whirring in my head and the pain I carry in place of all the belongings I left behind.

I feel like I am filling the pages with pain. If I keep writing, this little book will grow so heavy that I will no longer be able to lift it. But what else can I do but write the weight of my heart? If I wrote only of the land we crossed without the imprint of our footsteps on it, there would be no place to enter the landscape. And we are here instead of in our homes.

We are gone, gone like the petals of the almond trees, one week so full of scent and the next scattered on the ground. We are gone, gone away. The list of the dead grows, names disappear.

I remember Mama telling me about the time when Sarah, only three then, vanished from her sight. Sarah hid herself so well my mother's heart fell to her knees. I feel as if my heart has fallen and I am dragging it behind me. So much loss. Count them, these spaces between my fingers, count. Our voices have been left behind. I hear them singing on the wind. The Sabbath still comes, even after we are gone. Listen, hear the sounds of petals falling.

May 3, 1492

Peñaranda de Bracamonte

As they rode away from the convent, towards Salamanca, Chava thought of the places they had passed through so far. Each village a country of its own, each finca a town, each mountain its own Sinai. Even the smallest houses, with no glass for windows and just one or two rooms inside, had a hearth where a family gathered, where they told stories or sang. She felt like a migrating bird, sent out too early in the season, sent away from where the sun was just warming her nest. Each day unfolded from shadow and still she was unsure of how to fly. They rode all day and arrived at another of Isaac's cousin's in the late afternoon. Weary and sore, they had a small supper and were in bed before it was completely dark.

The next morning, when she managed to open her eyes, her head felt stuffed full of clouds. There was gray all around her, as if she was actually in the midst of sky. She rubbed her eyes. Sarah was breathing beside her, the deep breath of sleep. Chava realized it was nowhere near morning. She lay as still as possible in the silvery dark. Here she was awake when she should be sleeping. Her body tired and her mind whirling. She thought of lighting a candle and writing in the journal but was afraid to wake her sister. Sarah without enough sleep was no joy at all. Instead she kept still thinking of the days to come. She imagined tomorrow's road, the sway of her horse along it. She closed her eyes again and the next she knew her sister was jostling her awake, calling her a sleep-in.

Sarah had washed already and put her cold hands on Chava's cheeks to startle her into wakefulness. Chava splashed her face at the basin and slipped into her day dress. They each helped the other with the ties. Since there was no mirror in the room, they tidied each other's hair, pulling it back and tucking it through itself to hold it away from their faces.

When they went downstairs Isaac was already at table, a bowl of warm milk and bread in front of him. He looked worried. A number of Guardia had come through the neighboring town at dawn looking for travelers. A neighbor, just returned from her son's house, had seen them. She stopped by knowing the family often had visitors coming through.

"We best leave soon," Isaac said, "we do not want to bring you any trouble."

"No," the old man said, "better you move at a leisurely pace. Remember, you are doing nothing wrong. You have the permission. You are returning to your studies, visiting family along the way."

"Yes, but…," Isaac started.

"But nothing, son, that is all there is."

"We don't want to draw attention to you."

"Oh, the attention has always been on us; they know well what we are and who we are. Do not fool yourself boy. There has never been a real ease with those of us who converted after the riots. They have never been able to tell the difference between the Anusim and the true Conversos. We did what we thought we must."

"But won't they come for you then?"

"They might or they might not. We have some decisions to make ourselves. Whether to stay and continue as we have, or to leave all this- our home, our lands, our neighbors. They have been good neighbors. Or

149

whether to stop any pretense and let ourselves be swallowed in the jaws of the church. A few more people eaten up for dinner, as if we never were anything but Christians."

"Do you think, cousin, they will just forget your family are Jews? Do you think they will let you be Christians? There is all the talk of old families and new families. And I have heard that Torquemada proposes a notion of "pure blood" going back generations."

"Well he will have a hard time of that, will he not? They say his great grandfather was a Jew. The King's own grandmother as well; and how many others have not wed into families where there are Muslims or Jews?"

"True. But some cover it better than others."

"And why is it," he turned to Chava and Sarah who had sat down, their hands cupped around the warm bowls of milk, "that your mother is not with you? I know your father has passed, may his memory be a blessing. But why did your mother stay behind?"

Sarah looked at Chava. "She will come, Señor, but is first ordering our home and belongings, being sure to place them where they will be safe. She believes the king and queen will change their minds. She believes the edict will be lifted." His eye brows cocked.

"Yes sir, she does" echoed Sarah.

"And you child?"

Chava responded in an overly polite voice, "I do not believe so sir."

He looked to Isaac, who shook his head no, and then to Sarah who said, "I believe it might be. I believe there is a good chance that it will be, but there is no certainty."

"And when will your mother come and who will she travel with?"

"You ask so many questions, Señor." Sarah spoke demurely, deflecting the attention from Chava who looked ready to pounce.

"It is only to know so I can help make my own decision about what is best to do."

Sarah said, "Have your breakfast, sister. I am sure you are hungry, and the kind sir knows we must be leaving. He knows we do not have the answers."

Isaac felt Sarah's foot kick him under the table. "We did not speak of it, sir. I am sure we will have word from her when we reach their Aunt and Uncles in Portugal."

They finished their breakfast and went to gather their things, taking their leave politely and cautiously within the hour. They stopped once the house and village were out of sight. "Sarah, I was troubled by his questions."

"I know, something made me feel very uneasy."

Isaac said, "I know they are family, but not close, and there is something that did not feel right. I think their conversion may have been a deal made to protect just them. I think they will stay here, and I think it will cost them."

"I think it will cost us." Chava said and turned her horse toward Salamanca.

CHAVA

Now I comprehend a bit more of what my mother meant when she said she was tired. All those days of making the decisions, where we would go and how we would get there. She would rub her hand across her forehead as if it could soothe away the weight she felt. I knew the tiredness from carrying baskets of wheat when we would go to help on the finca. But that was a different tired. That was the body worn and sore from work. This weariness is very different. It does not come from using muscle and bone in the way they were meant to be used, but rather in not using them, and overusing our thoughts. Wearing a rut into the road of our mind, looking for a new direction when there is ultimately only one way to go, forward. I am worn, rubbed raw, bereft of any new ways of looking at our predicament. Tired like Sisyphus with his stone. Deeply vanquished in a way I had never been before. And I understood the looks on the faces of beggars we had passed in the street, of the waves of lost sorrow that must have drifted after the curse of the plague, of my mother's deep loss of the children who died before they were born, and even heavier in her arms, those that died before they could walk.

What sorrows we carry on the edge of our arms, the curve of our lips, in the muscle of our heart. How do we bear such loss and yet get up and walk, and even smile at the flitting of a wren? How are we made to do such things, to see weariness in everything, and sense a new beginning all at the same time? This new kind of seeing, this knowing, in the space between my bones, between my heart and the next breath I take, really knowing that I will never be home again. I will never again be a girl held on one side by my father's love and on the other by my mother's. It is just Sarah and me. I am grateful for my sister. But we will have to learn a new way to lean on each other, a new way to keep strong. At least until mother joins us again.

May 4, 1492

They slept for the first time in hay, climbing into the mow of the barn after dark. They thought they would be welcomed openly as they were cousins on their father's side. But the family had found sponsors and converted just after the high holidays in September, long before the edict was even issued. Since they were such recent converts, staying with them would have been too suspicious. Still, they were cousins they could not turn family away. They snuck all five of them in and had them leave just as dawn was making its way into the sky. They sent them on their way with plenty of food, apologies and well wishes. It made it all feel more and more real as if their lives really could be in danger.

There were more bird songs each morning, a fluttering of notes following them. Chava was never good at recognizing the different songs, or forms of flight, though Sarah had a knack for both and could say which bird was which from the first cooing of the doves to the last dip of swallows in the evenings. The birds were returning even as they were leaving. Some stayed all year, but others wintered in Africa, or on the coast along Al-Andalus, where the weather was mild. Not like winter in Toledo, above the icy river, the fog gray and cold in the mornings. What bird would want to sing then?

The sun rose earlier, and the nights grew shorter as each day on the road became longer. After a week, it almost seemed that it had been this way for months. Only her dreams, especially those close to her waking, were filled with home. So, she carried the strands with her through the morning until, by midday, they were scattered along the way. Toledo filled her dreams while the sway of the horses filled her days, hearing the voices of the marketplace, or the discussion from her father's study about a passage in the Torah, heated between him and a few of his colleagues. Sometimes she would wake to some sweet strains of a song in Arabic strummed on a lute.

CHAVA

I wanted to stop, to let go of worrying, of counting steps and days. I didn't want to calculate the best path to take, nor wonder what the outcome of this or that would be. Stop. Rest. I want to watch the stars begin to appear, first one, and then another, a slow unveiling of the heavens, without thinking which direction we must go tomorrow, or watch the sun rise, the colors tint the sky, light awash through the last of the night to change what was unseen to the color of rose. And then by the time for market, you have already forgotten the dark. To measure a day in slowly done chores and lessons, in meals and conversations, instead of the distance placed between myself and home. I have traveled before, of course, with Papa and even with the whole court and felt the gaiety that comes from things newly seen. But this is so different. There is not gaiety here; it is, step after step, carrying me away.

Even though I know that the stars are the same ones as in Toledo, we have not journeyed so far. Though I know this, when I look up at night, I find myself thinking how different it all looks. Surely the constellations themselves have changed. In the old Greek stories someone is always chasing after someone else until they are redeemed, placed into the sky forever, immortalized by their pantheon of gods. I never learned Greek but know the stories from the Arabic and even helped translate some into Castilian. I told a few to the housekeepers' children and then they looked at me so wide-eyed as if the stars themselves were make believe. Perhaps they are. Perhaps they are not there at all and we just think we see the great expanse of night opening up as the sun slips away. I think, for a moment, that this is all just a dream but wake then, not really rested. I wake and make ready to start again. We are traveling towards some sense of freedom, but it is the exile I am carrying with me. It does not let me rest.

I think perhaps I did not love it all well enough. My home, the view from the window, my mother's voice, my father's words. And not just those closest to me, but the others who surrounded my childhood, my aunts and uncles, cousins, neighbors. I unwrapped the small scented amber that my aunt had given me years ago, wood and moss. A scent she always wore and gifted me. The things I will never see again. I cannot begin to count them. And yet, I carry them with me.

It was the second time I overheard them when they thought I was not near enough. I never thought of Sarah and Isaac as separate from me, separate, but together. It is not that they were whispering secrets to each other. No, nothing like that, but their words wrapped around each other with such ease that I felt excluded.

Sarah said, "Isaac, can you imagine in five years from now this will all be something that we will think of as a story that happened to us?"

Isaac said, "Think back five years, can you not remember the shining plates at Seder, can you not remember your papa and my papa arguing after the dinner about homelands?"

A silence followed that I knew was filled with Sarah shaking her head and a smile appearing just before the intake of breath that I could hear. Oh yes, I know my sister.

"Of course," she said, "but that was repeated every year until this one, the polished silver and the days of cooking and the story and then the long drawn out discussions about what next year in Jerusalem meant."

"Stubborn men, our fathers." Isaac said.

"Oh, and we are nothing like them." Sarah laughed.

With Isaac she laughed so much more easily than with me. Sometimes I felt they were angry with me for the situation we were in- for the leaving, for the walking, for the tiredness in our legs and hearts. At least those are the thoughts that ran through my head when I heard them laughing together. But when I came around the corner, not wanting to keep myself where they could not see me, afraid perhaps of what I would hear if I did, they welcomed me with open faces.

"Sister," said Sarah, "we were remembering the Seder. I was trying to imagine what it would be like for that to be an absence in our lives."

I replied, "Maybe it won't need to be absent, just different; maybe we can keep what we loved best and discard what we didn't."

"Oh," said my little sister, "but I loved everything best." Isaac and I laughed. For a moment she looked so young, but none of us were children anymore. Indeed, we were no one's children anymore, it was just us and we would need to take care of ourselves, and each other.

It felt good to be drawn into their talk. It is too easy for me to exclude myself, to feel the weight of responsibility on my back alone, and I have no need to do this. I must remind myself. I have no need at all to be the dependable one. I need to step back and let Sarah and Isaac take it up as well. Otherwise, I know that as my muscles harden with the effort and my face screws up in the concentration, I will become hard inside myself. I don't want that. I have so many dreams yet, so many things I want to do.

May 5, 1492

Chava knew it when the weight gathered in her lower belly in the morning. When they stopped for their dinner under a lone ash tree she felt the flow as she dismounted. She took the small bag from inside her saddle bags and went back to where the land sloped down and afforded some privacy. Sarah watched her and met her as she came back up the hill.

"Are you well sister?"

"Well enough," Chava answered, "it is something I thought about but did not think through." Sarah nodded realizing her own time of month would follow very soon, as it always did.

"I just don't know how to manage the washing staying in someone's home or, G-d forbid, an inn. I only have so many strips. I wish we were home."

And Sarah reached for her hand. It was usually Chava comforting her but this time it was Sarah who said, "We are home as long as we have each other." She reached up to pull her sister's ear gently, an old sharing from their childhood meaning that all would be well.

But then the real weightiness fell on them both and Sarah said, "It makes me realize something I had not really thought about. We will never enter the mikvah of our Toledo. Now I understand better what Mama spoke about. Do you not remember the conversation we had soon after we decided we would leave? Mama said that when she was a young group of women would gather on the Sabbath. While the men were arguing the broader laws of Torah, the woman parsed out the laws of daily life.

Sarah added, "Mama said the women understood the difference between the ideal of what is written and the real of what must be lived. You will not be able to keep kashrut when you are traveling, and perhaps not even in the land you arrive in to call home. But if your hearts and your intentions allow for the greater truths, then that is the same. And as for the mikvah, for cleansing after your time and for keeping yourself separate, that too will be unlikely.

But remember the greater truth, the intention behind the rule, to have a time of some rest, sometime apart from the ordinary, and then to reenter the ordinary with some ritual. There are those that follow word for word what the Torah says and think that brings grace. But paying attention to the spirit of what is written, that is the real grace. Men often have a harder time understanding the difference between the meaning of the word and the promise it carries. Some women do, too. There are those that see the sky as only sky but do not hear the stories the stars sing."

"That was it exactly Sarah, word for word. Tonight, when we stop, will you help me remember Mama's words so I can write them down in the book Mama gave me?"

When they came back under the tree Isaac had spread a blanket and put out the food their host had packed for them the night before. Sarah and Chava both laughed at the sight of him bent over, something he never would have been caught doing at home- setting the table for two girls. He righted himself and stood and bowed,

"Welcome to the house of Isaac", he said formally.

Already the way they were doing it was different from how they had done things before. They sat down to cheese and bread and peppers and olives. Their host had been kind and known not to send chorizo or jamon with them. He spared them as some would and some would not along the journey. As they ate, Chava thought about the stories of her mother's family's exodus from Montpellier two generations earlier. Her mother often talked about the mikvah in the quarter; she could describe it as if she had known it herself. The steps leading into the room, the flickering candles, the stones from hundreds of years before her grandmother's time. The way the indentations held the feet of girls becoming women and women carrying babies. How each indentation was different and marked with so many feet carrying so many women and their hopes. The cleansing she had told her girls about was not to make them clean but to make them free. Isaac listened carefully.

They were quiet there under the tree. Each of them in their own thought. Isaac watched them thinking. There was so much he did not know about these girls, though he had known them all his life. They were so much stronger than him, he thought. And he wondered if they knew this or not. What he also did not know was that in the same bag where Chava carried the strips for her monthly time was wrapped something very precious. Something worth more than any other gold or jewel they carried with them and something that must be guarded; it was not only their future but the future of knowing the rituals of always. Her mother had given it into her care, the special prayers to the Shekinah, the rituals to follow at Rosh Hodesh and in the cycles of a woman's life.

May 7, 1492

Salamanca

Leila's walk gentled Chava into daydreams, remembering the stories her father told of his time studying in Salamanca. As a boy, it had been a dream of his to come to the university here. There was a brief time that he thought he would like to study medicine, but he was always drawn back to languages. It ran deeply through his family. He believed that in order to know words you had to know the stories behind them. He convinced his father to let him come and study philosophy here in order to give depth to his Greek and Latin. He entertained us with renditions of songs that he and his fellow students sang.

Benjamin still had ties with the small community of Jewish families as well as with some of the scholars, like Don Zacuto who had invited them to stay. Their father had visited him many times. He said that Zacuto and Colon had spoken and Zacuto had advised him and given him maps showing the best routes to take.

Señor Zacuto was an important link in dispersing some of the manuscripts they carried. They arrived in the late afternoon as the light was beginning to change, turning the city golden. Isaac gave them the message immediately and they assured him they knew.

Don Zacuto and his family would be leaving soon for Lisbon. He asked them to carry some other documents to Oporto as their uncle had readied transport to other places. It was a great net of exchanges extending through Europe and Africa and the Ottoman Empire all the way to the Holy Lands. This document traded for that one; this manuscript to be sent all the way to Cairo, another to Fez. It was its own diaspora of knowledge, a way to assure that this legacy of learning arrived to the communities safely, so it could be used and preserved.

Sarah and Chava had been to the home of the Zacuto family before. While their areas of study may have differed, her father and the professor had much to share, not the least of which was a love of wine and a love of argument. Benjamin found his ways through words and Zacuto through numbers. But they both sought deeper understandings, a way to transform what was in front of them, opening gates to new understandings. Chava had loved to listen to them argue, even more to listen to them dream. There were arcs to words, and arcs to numbers, like bridges that created spans to other places. And now, here they were arriving as the family was making ready to leave. As if they had already left, as everyone would be leaving. Some were packing to leave Spain while others were sealing their lives up, leaving everything they knew without leaving their homes. It seemed there was no longer any way to stay.

Don Zacuto gave Sarah and Chava his condolences and his apologies for not having been to visit them while they sat in mourning. His daughter was near in age to them; they had played together when they were little. She was recently married and had returned to the house of her parents to help them ready for the journey she would undertake with them. They brought in tea, sweetened with mint and sugar in the style of Andalucía, and little almond cookies. They sat together, Zacuto and his wife, his daughter, and Isaac and Chava and Sarah, all in the salon as if it were only a passing visit and not the last time.

The Zacuto family was bringing the astrolabe he had refined to the king of Portugal. The king had invited them to help the Portuguese explorations and to receive safety under his protection. It is not that there was complete trust with the Portuguese court, but it was not too far to go, and at least for now, secure. They spoke of how Esther and Isaac's parents still held hope for a relinquishing of the bans and a rescinding of the edict. But the professor told them he did not think it would happen. He thought Isabel was too entrenched in her decision. While it was possible the king might soften, it was the queen's final decision. Fernando would not go against her on this; it seemed Torquemada held more sway.

Zacuto spoke about the time, not so long ago, he had met with the king and queen to tell them of the new astrolabe. He knew about Colon's pleas for backing and how useful the instrument could be to the endeavor. But Torquemada had dissuaded the royals, saying that it was an instrument of Satan, as Zacuto was a Jew and could not possibly have their best interests at heart, nor the best interests of Spain. At first Fernando tried to push off Torquemada's words as nothing but taunting, but the Inquisitor became more and more adamant. When it was obvious that there would be no possibility of a serious talk, the king made a time to meet with Zacuto later, and alone.

But within hours Zacuto received a message that the king could not attend him, and indeed would not be able to for many days. He knew then that Torquemada had succeeded. Zacuto returned to Salamanca and already there were swirls of rumor of what was to come. Considering how Fernando would not meet with him, Zacuto decided he would contact the king of Portugal sooner rather than later, and so secured safe passage. He would take with him some of the manuscripts they had brought with them out of Toledo. His connection to the king of Portugal assured safe passage and ease, especially given how much the tools of navigation interested the Portuguese court.

They stayed in Salamanca with the family for three days, enjoying the feeling of being at home. They observed Shabbat there and stayed until the Monday morning. They left feeling more rested than they had since departing from Toledo. It would be two days journey to Mieza, the village that would be their last stopping point in Spain. It seemed as if they were already at the end of their journey though, in truth, they were still very much at the beginning.

May 9, 1492

Waking in the upstairs room at the finca, near Vitigudino, the air was filled with the song of thrushes and the scent of earth. In her own Toledo the morning sounds were of footsteps and horses' hooves, of voices drifting up from the early vendors at the market, and in the occasional stillness, the trailing end of a bird's call, the bleating of sheep crossing the fields outside the city wall. But here in the midst of neither town nor village, the sounds of birds turned the air to a rousing chorus as the sun lightened the sky.

"Sarah, are you awake?" She nudged her sister and felt her stir.

"Sarah."

"Why do you always ask me if I'm awake when you know you are waking me up even as you ask?" Sarah spoke without opening her eyes.

"I wanted to talk with you." Chava brushed a stray hair back from her sister's forehead. Just as Sarah reached for her knee under the covers, Chava jumped. It was her most ticklish spot. It was the one way her little sister could always bring her to her mercy. They both laughed.

"I was awake, trying to catch the last wisp of a dream."

"What was it?"

"We were on a ship, a small one with oars, no sails, but it kept raising up above the water and each time the shore would grow more distant."

"Was it frightening?" Sarah drew closer to Chava.

"No. It was, I'm not sure exactly…alluring?"

"Alluring?!"

"Well, I was curious. It was me and a boatman, all covered in a cloak, and I could see you waving from the shore. Even though I got further away, you stayed the same size. What do you think it means?"

"That the journey may be longer than we expect, but that we will be together."

"Ah little sister, you are so wise in the morning." And she reached for the inside of Sarah's wrist, her most ticklish spot. Sarah managed to twist away and grab for a pillow. She hit her sister and feathers tumbled over them both." They gasped with laughter.

Suddenly Chava grew quiet, "Do you think we will see our mother again?"

"What are you saying Chava? Mama said she would join us before the time is out."

"I woke with a heavy feeling and the sound of mother's voice saying goodbye. It was not a dream, more of a remembrance. It felt so final to me."

"I think she will come. When has she ever broken her word?"

"Never, when she was the one in charge. But just like she whispered it would all be all right when father died, and it wasn't, now she says she will join us. She might not be able to."

"You are letting your fears get the best of you. Chava. You are always thinking of every possible outcome, except the easiest one."

"Don't be angry with me. Of course, you are right. It is only me turning things around in my head until I make a mess of them."

"Speaking of messes, we would best clean this up."

They stuffed the feathers back into the pillow as best they could and feeling a bit sheepish, rose and pulled the covers back making everything look as neat as possible. There was a knock on the door and the girl who worked in the house brought warm water in a basin. They washed using the scented cloths that had been left on the bedstead the night before.

When they came down Isaac was already at the breakfast table and the Señora of the house rose to bid them good morning. The kitchen girl brought warm milk and bread, honey and cheese. They ate with relish, complimenting their host on the food. They were on the road before the sun was too high. The sky was clear, and it looked to be an easy day of travel.

Chapter Ten

The Edge of Spain

Mieza de la Ribera

Chava's journal

From the balcony the view is toward the river. On Sunday when the morning bells sounded from the church. I could hear the people gather in the square. I could feel all the week's work, the dirt, the tiredness, lift from their shoulders.

On Friday we lit the candles. The fields were beautiful, drenched in late spring flowers. On a rock ledge that seemed like a table, jutting out beyond the cliff, we knelt down and put the candles between us, shielding them from the wind, or anyone's eyes. I took my handkerchief and placed it over my head; my sister did the same. I could not hear her cry, but I knew she was weeping. My poor Sarah. I wedged the candles into a rift in the rock; they fit perfectly. I whispered the prayers and longed for the fullness of a voice without fear. The wind held itself just a moment, long enough for the glow of the candles to light our faces, and then a gust blew them out.

When I was little, I asked Mama if everyone lit candles at the same time because, if they did, surely there would be so much brightness all at once G-d would have to come and see.

"He does." She said to me. But now there is darkness in those windows, and silence. We lose our rituals and our days lose their form. I make my heart strong so I will not lose the shape of myself.

Mieza lies at the very edge of Spain. The lanes leading out from town toward the cliffs and the River Duero below are lined with orchards and small well-tended fields. Chava grew up on the lemons, honey and cherry preserves sent by their cousins. The family had roots in many places. Her father often said, "Hundreds of years in Sevilla, hundreds too in Las Arribes. And before that it was all so long ago it is only remembered in prayers." Her father's family had come to Spain from Judea in the times of the Romans. They were traders and translators, doctors and advisors. They always lived close to those in power, advising and interpreting, but of course never ruling. Whatever lands they owned were far flung like the ones in Mieza. Their family spread and scattered like seed until someone found a hold in the soil and could grow something more permanent, than the wind that carried them.

ESTHER

When I was pregnant with Sarah, on the days when there was no rain, I would take Chava past the gates of the quarter and meander down to the river. Chava loved to see if her stones would make circles when she tossed them. She stood as close to the bank as I let her. She had no fear of falling into the water. When she tired of throwing stones, we sat and watched the river birds dip and dive for fish. Not yet two years old, she could name at least five by kind and size. Chava always liked to categorize and sort, trying to contain in some small way the world that fell out before her. I could feel the baby turning slowly inside me. I would pray that this one would be born healthy, like Chava. I did not think I could bear to lose another child. And yet, not quite sixteen years later, the shadows of my girls are falling someplace far away from me.

I picture them on the road coming into Mieza, a road I know well. No one would imagine, as they approach the town, that just on the other side the land slips into a canyon and the sky falls away. The cliffs leading down to the river are terraced on both the Spanish and Portuguese sides. Looking up you often see the wide wing span of the storks that nest there. They return in the spring of each year.

Somehow the way the winds blow and catch the rain creates small patches of warmth, producing a more southern climate. There are lemon trees and almond groves not usually found so far north. In the spring, the trees are in full flower-white and pink adorning the greening hillsides. There is a beekeeper with the sweetest honey and stands and stands of olive trees. And vineyards of course, the old vines thick as my wrists. Benjamin and I used to talk of living in Mieza. Time there is the rotation of the seasons.

Just some years ago, they found the statue of a Virgin floating in the river. They carried her up and took her to be the town's patron saint. They lovingly restored her and placed her in the church. On feast days she is brought out to great ceremony. Near Easter she is paraded through the town, draped with wreaths of almond flowers. There is music then and dancing. We were always welcomed to join the festivities.

CHAVA

We have arrived in Mieza. It took so long in some ways and yet, in others it seems just yesterday I was sitting at the window seat daydreaming. The rains and the days on horseback all blend together- sometimes like a song, other times a cacophony of lament. Not that any of us wept past that first day. We knew if we let ourselves give voice to the grief that hammered inside, we would never take the steps we needed to reach the Rio Duero. The day after we arrived, we walked the path outside of town that led to the descent to the river and the crossing. We walked it slowly, each of us thinking of the leaving to come. The final steps that would take us away from our land and set us in another. The river was the boundary between countries and kingdoms, but too it was the line between what we thought our lives would be and what we would have to make of them now.

Today we were only to mark the distance, to see across to where we were heading. To alleviate the tension of waiting and to seem as if we were doing something besides waiting. I suppose we were practicing. It would be nearly a week before our Uncle could send his boat to carry us down river to Porto. There were fruit trees along the path; the plots marked out by short stone walls. So many stones piled one on top of the other.

The quiet of our voices, our not talking, which was so much louder than our usual conversation, that easy banter between us since childhood. Almost like tossing a ball about the garden, or the weaving of string games. Now there was a thick silence as each of us visited our own sadness, our own trepidations. Perhaps we wanted to protect each other from the weight of our thoughts. But then we came around the final turn and the land dropped away to sky. The scent of the almond trees washed over us, blossoms filled with the light and seemed to move to the faraway rushing of water. It was beautiful. This earth that would bear the last steps in our homeland was so beautiful.

The way the flowers dropped from the trees, as if weightless, as if there was no air, as if they took an effortless leap, as if it were rest that each petal sought and rest that they were given. The petals lay soft pink under the clusters of almond trees, the first blooming gone; the fruit not yet grown. Just a week ago, the whole hillside had been a gossamer of flowers and the softest of perfumes filled the breeze. Now green fought for green and the nibs of fruit fought for light and enough of whatever it was that

169

coursed through the branches and limbs to bring them the nourishment they needed to grow.

I remember being here when I was a child. It was winter and all the lines of the terraced hillsides were clear and plain against the gray sky. I fancied it was giants who made the steps from the river to the town, down one side of the cliff face in Portugal and then up this side here in Spain. I convinced Sarah of it, then made her be the one to ask if it was true. The younger brother laughed, but the oldest bent down and took Sarah's hands and whispered, "Yes, how did you guess? It is a secret no one here wants to tell. We do not want anyone to know we had not done the work ourselves."

Sarah laughed and looked at me. I felt both gladdened and just a little bit ashamed, knowing it was not the truth, thinking of the women and men digging and digging in the sun and rain. I was proud for telling a story worth believing and a bit guilty to pull the wool over my sister's eyes. All these years later, I am thinking of those giants again and wishing they were real, wishing they would carry us down to the river and across. And then come back and shake the king and queen from their royal perches and throw Torquemada into the sea, past the pillars of Hercules. Wishing that then they would carry us back again and things would be as they were.

But the petals have fallen, strewn all along the ground, and I think about tears, and I know we have fallen from our home and there is nothing left to do but leave. We delayed our leaving in the hopes mother would join us.

We went down to the river to send a message to our Uncle. After dawdling on the long walk back, it was later than we had planned when we reached the house. We thought we would be late for dinner, but no one had sat to table yet. There were riders at the door, and they had a letter for us.

170

They bowed a farewell as we approached, and I stopped them and asked where they had come from. They answered Salamanca, and before, that Arevalo. The letter left Toledo on Sunday and has traveled fast to reach you. We were told it was of utmost importance. I had been thinking that it was a letter from Mama, but now I saw that the seal was not ours.

I thanked him and took the letter inside. Isaac and Sarah followed me. Our cousin told us to go ahead and open it, that they would wait dinner for us. I broke the seal and saw it was from the son of Abravenel. Your mother has come under scrutiny, it said. She did not wish to write you herself for fear the letter would be intercepted and bring suspicion on you. You are to go ahead and cross to your Uncle and Aunt as soon as you can. We will watch out for her safety, I promise. Sarah put her hand to her mouth to stifle a cry. Isaac's hand somehow went to the short dagger he always carried at his belt. I stood motionless, a million thoughts whirring through my head. How will I do this? How will I assure my mother's safety and our own? Oh, what do they know? And why, why now, when we are so close?

Julia came into the room and put her arms around my shoulder, "It is bad news?" She asked. I think the men must have told her something because she did not look at all surprised when I nodded my head and let the story stumble out. "Come. I know you are in shock. Please come and eat and we will talk."

I let myself lean against her and we followed her obediently to the table. Their girl served the soup and I cannot remember tasting it but the warmth of it felt good. We were tired from the walk to the river, and tired from the weeks of journey proceeding that. We were tired and now for the first time, I was also really frightened. I could feel the fright in the tendons around my bones. I could feel it sitting like stones in my stomach. When they came with the second course, I could not eat anymore. Gabriel looked at me and nodded.

"It is time to talk. Your mother is brave, trying to do what your father would have done, and she has done well. They will question her, but I am sure they will let her go. She has many friends at court." I listened but it was as if his words had to weave through a chorus that repeated itself again and again. I should be with her. I should be with her.

"I must go home." I said out loud.

"You cannot, there was another letter addressed to Julia. It was from Abravenel as well, but it contained you mother's wishes, asking that you do not turn back; that you take yourselves and the things you have brought and get across to Portugal. She knew you would want to go back, and you can't. Do you hear me, Chava?"

I nodded my head, but really saw myself shaking it no. No, I do not hear you. That is what I wanted to scream, but I kept my lips pressed tight.

Sarah had not touched anything on her plate either. "We will make it worse, is that it?"

"Yes, Sarah it will draw more attention than ever if you were to go all the way back. You can write her, but you must not mention this."

She nodded. Isaac asked if his parents had been questioned as well, and they had not as yet.

And then Sarah asked, "Why did you tell us?"

"To be honest child, I was considering not telling you until you were already across, and your Uncle had you safe in hand, but you came back with the horseman here. It would not do to lie to you."

"Omission is not a lie then?" I almost smiled. This was an argument my father and I had often engaged in.

Gabriel shook his head, "You are your father's daughter child. My primary concern is your safety. Tomorrow Juan and Jose will begin the return journey with your horses. The mules will stay behind. But children you must leave with haste."

That evening Chava saddled Leila and went out along the cliff edge, out past the pasture lands. She stopped under the changing sky, the slow dusk spreading towards her. She bowed over her horse's beautiful neck and buried her hands and face in her mane. She left her tears there, knowing Leila would take them home.

Chapter Eleven

The Crossing

Chava's journal

When we walked down the cliffs to the river, I cried. I bent down to pick up the last of the almond blossoms and pressed them into my hand. My sister reached for my hand and I put half the petals into my pocket and let the rest scatter in the breeze- as we are scattered, and as we are saved. I took my sister's hand and she smiled for me. Later, when I took the handkerchief mother had given me as we left, one my grandmother had embroidered, from my pocket. It had taken on the scent from the blossoms and a small stain. I shall keep it forever.

ESTHER

In the month since the girls had been gone, I worked with the old families, Abravenel and Seneor and Santangel. Each day brought less hope that the edict would be rescinded and with it more determination that the learning of near a thousand years would not be lost as well. With the reaches of cousins and profusion of languages and connections, manuscripts were sent to the communities to the south in Fez and to the east in the Ottoman empire. What they could not send, they hid. In the packages were keys to homes and documents of land ownership. There was a trunk loaded onto the ship that Colon was captaining.

But rumors were beginning to circulate that the day before the Benveniste brothers had been taken with the package bound for Salonica. I woke startled with an acrid taste in my mouth, reaching across the bed for Benjamin. There was only cold and when I looked toward the fireplace even the embers had died out. For a few minutes I lay listening, not quite sure of the time of day, knowing I was in my own bed but not quite piecing together why I was alone. I could not get the bad taste from my mouth- bitter, dry, cloying, as if I had swallowed a mouthful of ash.

I lay cocooned in the heavy covers and let the sense of things come back to me. Benjamin would never again warm my bed. It had been over four months since he was gone. I could still feel him at times but not nearly so clearly as in those first weeks when his presence pressed against my shoulder. Then while readying for the girls to leave I heard his voice, full of advice and guidance, and at moments, admonishments. I shared the advice with my daughters but kept his warnings to myself, especially about my staying instead of leaving with them for Portugal.

Chava and Sarah should be making the crossing into Portugal. Just yesterday I had word they arrived safely in Mieza. Oh, how I miss them. But what can I do now but continue what we started? There are only a few more manuscripts and letters to be sent safely out to the communities.

So much had come to us as one of the safe houses of keeping; the poetry and the science, the math and the letters from the sages, the Midrash and the translations of the Quran, the poetry and the pottery, which held perhaps the greater truths.

All my life I was schooled in the weight of words-how they carried voices and intonations. That is why the translations were so important. It was not just the content that needed to be carried into the other language but the tonality, the meaning under the meaning. Poetry is the most difficult to translate because of the breath that is carried in the line and how that changes when you change the words from one language to the other, still it is possible. I remember coming into my father's study when I was just a girl and listening to him reading the words out loud, back and forth, first in Hebrew and then in Arabic and then in French. Measuring the syllables and in breath finding the right weight to the line, seeking to carry the rhythm and the melody from one tongue to another.

I learned about the secrets of words, how the heft of them could change meaning, how the breath behind them could make someone think one way or another when they heard them said, or how the thickness of a written line could carry import over one that was scribed lightly. The difference of the way a hand held a pen could be the difference of the way the message was interpreted. So much depended on the width of words, the unspoken language within the language. These are the secrets the translator knows.

I felt the morning come and heard the sputtering of yet another rain through the chimney. It must have damped the fire and that must be why I woke with this taste in my mouth. The warmth of the room drowned in the sorrow of the skies. It had been a colder, rainier spring than I could ever remember. Some said it was the sadness brought on by the edict, by us being exiled in body and spirit from this place that had become home. Home, now there is a word for translating. All its different meanings and still I wonder if we have ever belonged anywhere. I heard then a knocking on the door and Maria's feet scuffling to answer it at this early hour.

"Is the señora in?"

It was a commanding voice. Maria answered saying I was still abed. The dawn had barely come.

"It is urgent." I thought I recognized the voice of Luis Santangel. But why would he be coming to my door and at this hour? He had been trying to keep his distance from the Jewish community since Torquemada had begun to question even the new Christian families of good standing. It was well known that some of his family had remained Jews and were planning to leave Spain in the coming month. He had been a stalwart supporter of the Jewish community even while being sure to keep a line drawn between us.

I rose then and put a robe around me tying it at the waist. I sought out my house shoes and dipped my fingers in the basin that had last night's water in it still. Maria came into the room looking concerned. I am sure my face must have betrayed the same worry as I saw in hers.

"It is Señor Santangel; he says he must speak with you. I have shown him to the library."

"Tell him I will be down promptly."

"He says it is most urgent señora."

"In a moment, Maria. I must gather my wits." I splashed my face with water and tucked up my hair, putting on a kerchief.

There was nothing for it. He would have to see me in disarray if it was so urgent, better still for me to go down than for him to come up, I thought. I took the candle Maria had left for me and went down the stairs. The house felt so large, so silent, with Chava and Sarah gone. It did not feel like my home, only the shell of it then, only that.

"Dona Esther," Santangel rose as I came into the room. I saw that Maria had already placed a log on the fire and a welcome flame leapt. I crossed the room to stand in front of it, feeling chilled even though it was nearing the middle of May.

"I am sorry to come so early. Forgive me."

"I know you would not if it were not urgent. Sit Don Luis, tell me what it is that brings you here?"

"I have not slept this night at all. I left the king nearing midnight. He was angry. He had been informed that the Jewish community was sneaking out wealth and documents. I do not know who has told him, only that he is upset. I went to speak to Abravenel with my brother. He confirmed the king's suspicions."

"But why are you here, Don Luis? You know my husband is long dead."

"Dona Esther, you and I both know you are as capable a business woman and translator as he was. Your name has come into Torquemada's list. Do you really plan on converting?"

"I have let it be known that I am seriously considering it. I have met with the priest, as you well know."

"Well it is time to make the consideration more than a thought…or it is time to leave, Dona Esther. I come as a friend. I come out of loyalty to your husband, to your family and to mine. I come with a warning. You are no longer safe. And I see how empty your library shelves are."

"What use have I for so many books with my daughters gone and Benjamin gone forever?"

"Do not try to be coy with me Dona Esther; we have known each other too long. You will not fool anyone. Your own knowledge can serve you or harm you."

Esther sighed, "How long do you think I have, Don Luis?"

"A day, maybe. I think you must decide today." He moved toward me then and took my hand. He kissed both my cheeks and looked at me and whispered, "I am sorry. I am sorry for all of this." And then he bowed and left.

May 14, 1492

They walked down through the crisscross path from terrace to terrace below the flowering almonds and lemon trees. The mules carried the trunks that held their clothes. The manuscripts carefully stitched under the lining, the handwritten pages of Maimonides, a treatise on astronomy, the poems of Rumi and Halevi, the old Haggadah, the first printed copies of the Torah from the presses of Guttenberg. For a family who lived by their words, these were more precious than the coins sewn into their seams and the jewels cross-stitched below their bodice. Chava carried too the works on the Shekinah that her mother had pressed into her hands, bidding her to keep them close. They were rare and very, very old.

They went slowly as the paths were muddied from the recent rains. The descent normally took no more than two hours, but the morning was beginning to stretch into the afternoon, and they were all growing anxious. Their aunt and uncle had promised to send someone to meet them at the crossing. Looking up they caught the shadows of two storks crisscrossing above the cliffs.

"What if they stop us and demand to see our papers?" Sarah turned around to ask.

"It will depend on whose men are at the crossing," Isaac said, "whether they are Torquemada's or Fernando's."

Chava shook her head, "Listen to me. We must act as Papa always taught us, as if we have a right to be where we are. They are our men at the border. We have the right to cross. We have the right to cross with the respect due our family and I have a seal of the king to prove it."

179

Sarah laughed then and gave her sister a kiss on the cheek. "Chava, if you could have seen your face just then, I think the queen herself would have curtsied to you."

And then, just as the dock was in sight, there was the sound of men coming up the path and suddenly blocking their way. "You are Chava and Sarah, the daughters of Esther of Toledo?"

"Yes," Chava answered. Isaac tried to step between her and the soldier, but he was yanked back by another. Sarah caught his eye and silently begged him to hold his peace.

"Why do you ask? We are going to our family in Porto; we have a right to cross. Look, the boat and my uncle's men are almost across the river."

"We saw them when we landed. You have the right to cross but you do not have the right to carry out coins or goods. They belong to the king and queen."

"What makes you think we are carrying anything?" Chava kept looking right into the soldier's eyes.

"Your mother has recently been arrested and questioned."

Chava felt her knees buckle then. Sarah let out a cry but put her hand over her mouth. Certainly, their mother had not converted yet and so they would not be able to question her, she still had more than a month under the law.

"I am sure you are mistaken." Chava said in the haughtiest voice she could muster.

"I am sure I am not," he drew a rolled document from his satchel, "you can read, I suppose?"

Chava took it and broke the seal. It was the seal of the Inquisition.

"Esther bet Deborah has been taken in for questioning regarding the smuggling out of goods that belong rightfully to the King and Queen of Spain and the Holy Father in Rome." Sarah was biting her lip to hold back her tears. Chava's hands were shaking so she pushed her nails into her palms to keep her voice steady.

"She will be released; it is false accusations." The oldest of soldiers looked at her, not without some pity.

The other boat was at the dock and a man rushed up the path toward them; her uncle himself had come. He was known here, recognized as a friend to the Portuguese king. The soldiers were readying to search the trunks, but he calmly drew out not only his documents assuring passage but a small bag of coins that caught the soldiers' eyes as well. The soldier who had spoken with Chava said, "I leave them in your charge, sir."

Chava began, "We have to go back Uncle; Mama has been taken."

Avram put an arm around each of his nieces, "I am so sorry my girls. You cannot go back. I will tell you once we are across the river. Come now, before they change their minds."

CHAVA

I wished I could bury my face in Leila's neck. I wish I was not stepping onto the flat boards of the Rabelo. I wish we were not heading away from home, ever further away. I could wish and wish, but all my wishing could not drown out Uncle's voice, or Sarah's quivering lip and silent tears, nor Isaac's hand gripped tightly into fists. I listened, but only with the part of me that could not help but hear. Uncle told us this in as a kind a voice as he could muster.

"Your mother has been taken into questioning. It is possible that she will be made to go in front of the king and queen, which means either they will hold her until the royals come to Toledo again, or that she will be made to go to the south to stand in front of them. Isaac, your parents are standing by her, but they have not been taken. They say because she is not a Converso, she is not charged with heresy. However, she most answer to not abiding the laws of the edict. By sending manuscripts and other items of import out of the country she is taking what rightfully belongs to the king and queen. They say she violated the provisions of the edict."

"But, how? And is not…"

"Let me finish Chava, there is more. Abravenel is speaking in her defense, Seneor as well. I do not know yet, for certain, but it is possible that Seneor will offer to convert if your mother and others are let go."

"I cannot believe he would do such a thing." Isaac shook his head as he spoke.

"We have had word from those close to him that he feels his time is near. He is 80 now, and that he sees this as an exchange, save one life and…"

Sarah responded reflexively, "And you save the universe." Uncle put his hand on her shoulder and with his other he reached for me.

"Under this saddest of circumstances, still I am glad that I am here with you."

By that time, everything was loaded and the ties had been loosened. We were moving toward Oporto, the river carrying us, almost as if we had to do nothing. Juan and Jose must be near to Vitgudino by now. The wooden boat glided along the river making hardly a sound. The cliffs rose on either side of paths weaving through terraces, almonds and lemons in flower. How could there be such beauty and such sadness at one and in the same moment?

We sat under an awning on pillows as the boatmen hoisted sail and steered us into the currents. The river was high this time of year and we would travel quickly. I surprised myself by falling into a hard sleep. Perhaps it was the lulling of the water or the duress of the crossing and the not knowing about Mama; perhaps it was that the movement, requiring no expenditure of any energy that lulled me as if I were a small child. I don't know, but I slept through until the afternoon. When I woke the hillsides startled me with how verdant they were. They were planted richly with vines and interspersed with lemon and olive trees, and everything was so green and lush and so full of this late spring. The altiplano seemed like something from a dream, the dry roads, the wheat fields we'd passed, the month of horseback, as we floated down the river toward the sea.

Chapter Twelve

In Exile

Oporto, Portugal

June 1492

The harbor at Oporto was noisy and crowded with ships from many places. They docked at their uncle's quay and stepped off to a carriage waiting to take them up the hill to his home. They arrived to hugs and tears from their aunt. Chava and Sarah had a room together with a large bed; the same room where they had often slept when they visited in the past.

The day after their arrival, they sat at the large oak table with their aunt and uncle and their cousin, their uncle and aunt's only child, visiting from Amsterdam where he had made his home some years ago, immersed there in commerce. Their uncle was more of a traditionalist than their father and he took Isaac aside to question him about the journey.

Chava overheard this and said, "Uncle, talk to us. Isaac is not our keeper. We are free women, or as free as any Jewish woman can be at this point in time. Remember we were raised to think and speak for ourselves." She saw a smile waver across her aunt's face.

"Yes Avram, you know our nieces have been well-schooled. They can think their way around anything you put in front of them."

He laughed then but reminded them this would not always be the case. They were both worldly and protected, brought up as they were, educated as they were; not all communities would honor that.

This is something they would need to consider as they thought about where they would move next. But enough of that, for now. Now they needed a time to rest, to find out about Esther's predicament and to catch their breaths. Everyone knew nothing would be the same again.

CHAVA

I thought I knew what would await us at the end of the road, but it seemed there was no end at all. The word of Mama's detention by the Inquisition and then her arrest pulled the ground out from under us. How could this possibly be? I could not picture my mama held in a cell, or questioned by irreverent men, held as if she were a thief or a traitor. I wanted to rush back again, but no one would let me go. And when another letter came from Mama, forbidding me to come to her, telling me that all would be lost if I turned around and came back into Spain, I had no choice but to stay on. Oh, how I grieved and how angry I was.

It did not help to see Sarah and Isaac so in love. The feelings they had held for each other were no longer secret and there had even been tentative conversations with uncle about being wed. I did not want to begrudge them this, but it added to my pain as if there was a vast cavern for me to hold all my hurt and all my grief, and only a slit of a window to let in happiness. As if these things could be measured like this. I should know better. Mama would want this for them, of that I was certain. She would want it for me as well, but I had no hope of feeling gladdened at all. I had memories when Daniel and I believed we had a future together but betrothed and beloved felt long ago.

Now I just felt old. My eighteenth birthday was approaching, and it looked like I would always be alone. Alone and without a real home. Oh, how heavy of heart I was feeling, how desolate. As if I were the great sea that Colon was crossing and the sky had gone blank of stars and there was nothing, nothing to guide me. The ground was roiling beneath me as I thought of Mama facing the Inquisitors, as I thought of Papa not even six months gone and my little sister trying to squelch her own joy, as mixed as it was with all the sadness.

When we first left Toledo, I have to admit there was a part of me that surged at the notion of an adventure. The three of us with no elders to point this way or that. Juan and Jose were Mama's eyes and ears on the trip, but still it felt like we had suddenly become the ones in charge and that the course we were setting was our own. Never mind that we had been pushed out, that our destination was set; there were the distances of the plains and the reach of the sky and the darkness outside of the towns that descended like the tapestries hung on the walls at home. But now, here in the safety of our aunt and uncle's home, with Mama ensconced in treachery of someone's doing and the world dropping away into the sea and some future I could not name or vision, I felt small and afraid and angry.

Papa always said that we were motivated by one of two things: love or fear. And that we had some choice in which of those two voices, often present at the same time, we would choose to guide us. I tried hard to listen for the words that came from love, but they were being strangled before my ears could catch their sounds. It was a pounding that seemed to drown all else and I felt myself short of breath. I was not so used to being afraid.

The sun came slowly down and lit the sky behind us with the vast range of blues I think of when I think of the sea. These waters of the Atlantic are so different from those of the Mediterranean. The Mediterranean reaches out to the lands we know and the Atlantic crosses to the places we know so little about, past the Azores and the Canaries. I wonder at the depths of the sea, at what the water holds in the time and

186

distance it carries. Long ago I am told our ancestors journeyed west from the lands around Jerusalem. Fleeing or searching? It seems like we have inherited that fate so often. I prefer the notion of searching. We are always seeking something. A way to make the day fuller, to make our lives feel rich, not with things but with a connection to the texts, to each other.

My mother carried stories with her that she inherited from her grandmother, just as my father did. I hope I can remember the stories well enough to pass them on, the murmurs of song. There was a lullaby my mother sang often, about the stars guiding David, and another my father would sing us in Arabic, that he learned from his grandmother from a time when we lived much closer together than we do now.

I wish sometimes I was born in that time when poetry was exchanged like bread and the voices of singers mixed the languages from verse to verse, the stories twisted like spun yarn making a pattern. At night the stars tell stories the old Greeks made up to explain the way the heavens moved. I wonder how Ulysses guided his ships from port to port. Father always said he did not have the advantage of the mapmakers and the astrolabe and so his journey took so much longer than he thought. I wonder if Colon knows the tales of Ulysses and is setting out on the same long journey but with no Penelope to await his return? Only kings and queens eager for the gold, always wanting more, willing to set ships out across the unknown seas in search of it.

August 1492

In late July, as the numbers of Jews trying to leave Spain grew and panic began to mount, Avram learned that Kemal Reis and his fleet were sent to Cadiz to take charge and transport as many people as they could.

Soon after a letter came delivered by a merchant. It was in Esther's hand, dated July 27, addressed to both Chava and Sarah at their uncle's house. They were so relieved to see a letter from her that before they even opened it, they jumped up and down and hugged each other, just as if they were still young girls. Sarah said to call their uncle and aunt to read it, but Chava grabbed her hand and headed to their room. They sat on the small window seat and opened it. Chava read it aloud to Sarah.

My darling daughters,

I know you are safely with your aunt and uncle. I am so thankful for that. I am sending this with a merchant headed to the Algarve and then to Oporto. He has promised me it will reach you within the month. I am so sorry my children, but I waited too long to leave Toledo and had to come south. Isaac's parents waited with me as well and we will sail together. We came all the way to Cadiz. There were many people on the roads. I thank G-d for your father's many connections. We secured the journey from Toledo to Cadiz with a merchant who traveled surely and quickly. We arrived in just over a week, though the way was hard. It felt like there was a multitude at the docks, trying to secure passage away. There is only a week now before we must be gone. Too many have waited and there are not enough ships. There are many wanting to profit, and they are charging great sums for a little piece of deck. But we have just heard from your Uncle's old

friend Kemel Reis. He was in Tangiers with a

small fleet of trading boats and is coming to take many of us who would

otherwise be stranded here. I know it means I will not join you for some

time yet, but at least Isaac's parents and I will leave Spain together.

I imagine you are anxious for all the details of my travails with the

Inquisition. They did not harm me, children. I am fine. It is only this delay

that they cost me, nothing else. I know I gave you a fright, but they let me go

and everything we could have wished for was secured, only I did not get to

leave with the time necessary to join you. It is a long story and I cannot

recount here. Know that I am sending you a package via a trusted source. It

should arrive before the new year.

I will write you when we have crossed the Mediterranean and we will

make plans. I imagine, from what your uncle said, you will be in Oporto for

a good time until he is able to move you all to Amsterdam. G-d willing, we

will have Passover together next year.

Sarah, you know I have given my blessing for you to wed Isaac, as

have his parents. The world is changing so quickly you need not wait the

full year from your father's passing. He would want you to begin again.

When you are ready, you should wed. Your uncle will see to all the

arrangements.

I entrusted the house to Maria. Chava, I have given Leila to Juan, as

well as the other horses. He will take charge of the lands. In order to be

sure that no one else would usurp our home, I signed over the deed to

Maria for the house and the deed for the lands to Juan. I trust them and

they have both sworn to me that should we return, dare I say when we

return, they will sign it all back to us. At least I am grateful that I know who

189

is in our home. Maria's daughter and her children will come to live with her, so there will be laughter in the hallways. I like to think of that.

I have with me the tablecloth we always used for Passover. The candlesticks I could not bring so I left them in the house. I left some other things as well, children, in the place where Sarah liked to sleep as a child. I must hurry to give this to the merchant. Tomorrow we sail just in time, my daughters, just in time. All my love.

Always yours,

Mama

CHAVA

We were so happy, we ran to find our aunt and read the letter to her and then, that night at dinner, to uncle and Isaac. Sarah and I took turns with the reading as if it were a Seder. It was the first time food tasted so good since we had left Toledo. Aunt had roasted a chicken with honey and rosemary and lemon, and the taste was sweet and full of spring.

Uncle traded often enough with Kemil Reis, had visited him in Istanbul, and trusted him well. We began to make plans and to talk of the future. Our cousin told us about Amsterdam in detail, the shops and the canals. We went to sleep happy that night thinking that we would all be together. Sarah and Isaac said they would wait to wed until mother and his parents arrived and we would have occasion then to celebrate something after giving away so much.

I fell asleep thinking how proud mother must be to have accomplished what she set out to do. I imagined father, resting now, satisfied his family would be safe and the manuscripts preserved. I had shown uncle and aunt all that I had brought with me except the one small book mother had especially entrusted me with, only Sarah knew of that. I vowed I would begin to read it again tomorrow and to work on translating it from the Hebrew into Castilian. I wanted to share it with other women, but first I would have to study it and understand it myself.

We had a week of happiness until another letter reached us, sent to my uncle in the hand of Kemil Reis himself.

My old friend,

I hardly know where to begin, but I must offer you my deepest condolences. Your sister-in-law and friends were on another vessel when the storm rose quickly. I thought they would be more comfortable on that ship. There were good sailors manning her, but the storm was too much, and the ship faltered. We tried our best. I am so very sorry. No one survived.

How different that supper from the one just the week before. We did not eat. I do not remember what was served. Sarah and I stumbled up to bed before it became dark and held each other as we wept. Isaac was away that day and we dreaded having to tell him when he returned. Our cousin had left that morning for Amsterdam before the letter had come. We were stunned into silence. It seemed as soon as we readied ourselves to be happy, to draw contentment from all of us being able to be together, even as we forsook our homes, that we were ripped apart with grief yet again.

And I could not help myself. I kept imagining that mother somehow survived, that she found some piece of a mast to cling to and rode out the storm, that she would wash up on some shore and kind people would find her and nurse her to health and then she would get word to us. When I tried to tell this to Sarah there was a moment when I could see her eyes flash with the possibility of a smile, but then she got angry with me. Do not do this Chava. Do not make hope where there is none. Do not lead me to believe what is not possible. Stop, please stop. And then she hugged me and we both cried more.

Up until now I had kept some thin silver strand of belief in G-d. Up until now I thought this must all be for a reason. Up until now I had some semblance of trust with the Almighty, but no more. I would keep this to myself. I would look for answers in the book mother sent with me, but I would not ask for anything in my prayers.

We sat Shiva for them, and then observed the 30 days of mourning, which came to an end just as Rosh Hashanah began. On Yom Kippur the Kaddish was intoned with all of their names. In nine months, in the time it would take a child to grow, we lost our home and our parents.

And still we were luckier than most. We had each other, our aunt and uncle. Sarah and Isaac would wed the next year.

Rosh Hashanah came late this year, at the very end of September. As if it was waiting to start a new year until we had finished mourning our parents. We were not finished but began to integrate that loss and grief into our daily bread. When I braided the challah for Rosh Hashanah, I thought of the three strands of sadness- our parents' deaths, the loss of our home, all that we would never be able to share. It was that last that would bring the tears smarting at the corner of my eyes, and the tightness to that soft place at the bottom of my throat. I would never enter my courtyard again, never ride Leila, never go the Mikvah with my mother, never hear my father's voice, never, never, never.

And then I would look at the flour on my hands as they stopped in the midst of making the Challah and I would think I have this- this scent of dough, this sun coming in at the kitchen window, my sister's voice as she comes in from the garden with the late greens in a basket, my uncle and my aunt, Isaac and who knows what else. Perhaps that was the thing that most brought back my breath, that unknown, that something more awaited us. That the world would open and open again and I would somehow step into it.

The package arrived three days before Yom Kippur. A small crate. It was addressed just to Sarah and me and so my uncle pried it open but did not lift the lid. He left the kitchen then, leaving my sister and me to open it in privacy. There are two shawls inside, ones that Sarah and I had loved, and inside each there were bound books, two of mother's journals, a letter for each of us, and there were the mezuzahs. One from the front door of our house and another from the kitchen door, as well as the ones from each of my grandparents' homes. I pictured then the dent in the door frames where they had been. I pictured the doors of our house shut and was eased with the thought of Maria opening it, and her grandchildren playing in the courtyard.

Sarah read her letter and then took Mama's shawl and wrapped it around her. I could tell she was not yet ready to share it with me. That was all right. Mama wanted me to know how much she thought of me and how she hoped I would find a love like she and Papa had. This is part what she wrote me.

My dear Chava

If anyone can make an adventure of this, my child, you can. Remember to fill the journal I gave you. We are a people that carry our stories, our history, as if it were this morning's bread. We take sustenance from it.

Someday you will write of these dark times when we are being thrown from our home yet again. Cast into wind and buffeted up against the mountains, made to cross waters and settle yet again. My daughter you will tell your daughters and sons and then they will write it down and someday my great-great grandchildren will know this house in Toledo as if the stairs and stones had echoed their own footsteps. Carry our love with you child. Let it be a whisper. Let it be a shout; know that it is always with you.

Always

Mama

Chapter Thirteen

Amsterdam, 1494

Chava's journal

The narrow streets let the winds pass through, the stones remain. The stones always remained. They hold the mark of hands touching the walls a last time, indentations of memory. Footsteps heading away, echoes gone. Only the wind in the streets that were once full of people calling out to each other, only the wind now remains. What you leave when you leave is not just a place but a life, a way of being in the world. What changes is what always changes. One century laments the last, the escape traded for the homes, the homes traded for the wanderings, one kind of safety traded for another kind of safety. One set of questions traded for another set of questions. The answers still wait be to be found.

CHAVA

The rhythm of the days eludes me here in Amsterdam. The mornings have a harsh chill as the sun seems to take its time in rising. People jostle down by the quays, walking quickly, barely stopping to say good day, to inquire after a neighbor. There is a word in Dutch that sounds like a grunt. I know it means pardon, but there is no grace in it. In my Toledo, people only asked pardon of G-d or the king and only for something serious. To each other they laughed if they collided on the street, and if they recognized you it was the beginning of a conversation instead of an apology given in such a rush. I find so little grace in anything here. Perhaps the paintings, the ones that succor light and let it move out from a corner, as if everything is waiting for its touch of warmth. But then, that is probably just me, waiting for a touch of warmth which does not find me, no matter how fine the room or how soft the cloth.

I have heard the stories of how difficult it was for Isabel to attain the throne. How, as a young girl, she was kept locked away in Arevalo and then once she and her brother were brought to court they were not allowed to leave again. How it must have pained them both to think of their mother locked away, unwell, seeing apparitions with no comfort. How, after her brother's wife bore a daughter, the line for succession went to her even though it was rumored she was not his. How Fernando and Isabel married in secret, supported by my father's friends. It was told that theirs was a real love, pledged and true, unlike most of the marriages between royals. Even so, kings and queens moved their children like pawns on a chessboard in order to arrange the best endgame that they could.

My own mother and father had real love between them. We were all that our family had and we, both Sarah and I, felt treasured. While mother and father would arrange our matches, we were assured always that neither of us would be forced to marry someone we did not want to. My parents joked how they would have our children to run in their gardens and that the swing my father had built for us would endure to their great grandchildren's time, even if they did not.

They will never know their grandchildren and our children will never know the house we grew in. There will be only stories of a garden and paths leading down to the river. Only imaginings of all that the great library in our house once held. There will be no window seat for my own daughter to daydream upon, no swing at the edge of the garden. No fields to visit, no streets to run down to finish an errand. I do not know what there will be. I

196

only hope I will one day have children who are loved and able to feel as safe as Sarah and I did when we were small. Indeed, as we did even as we came of age.

When we were little, and it was gloomy and cold outside, Mother would play a game with us. She said her father had played with her. She would ask, "How can you be somebody's blessing?" Sarah and I clamored to be the first to name something, but she would put her fingers to her lips and say, "Go, go and do it and then come back and tell me."

I would run to the kitchen to hug Maria and tell her how much I loved her soups. Sarah would run to find Juan and tell him how much she loved the flowers from the garden he brought us in the summer. Then we would both run back to find mother, arriving usually right at the same time. She would nod and smile and give us each a kiss on our forehead and ask how did that feel? And then send us from the room again.

Looking back, I realize she was trying to get her accounting done or was perhaps working on a translation or writing a letter. But she never just shooed us from the room; rather, she gave us the gift of knowing what it was to bring a smile to someone's face on a gloomy, wet day.

I try to remember to do that here in Amsterdam where it is so often gloomy and wet. Although now it is me at a desk working at a translation or, more often lately, trying to help another banished person from home find passage to someplace for which they are better suited. We have been here for a year now. I continue to live with Isaac and Sarah, but already I have begun to dream of someplace else. Now that I know mother will never join us, that our home is gone forever, I want to be away. I dream about crossing the sea and hearing the birds on those islands rumored to border the Indies. I know others believe there is no passage and that it is just a restless and untamed place, but I imagine flowers and birds and the sea washing on shores without buildings, without the weight of stone, the way my heart feels. And I want the sun of someplace new and bold.

I am tired of the heavy days and the burden of courtesies. The truth is my own heart is broken and I do not think it will mend in this flat, wet land where commerce surrounds everything. I miss the shifting seasons of home, the flowering trees of Spring that give way to the coming heat, the dry summers the land gone to shades of ochre and rust under a vast uncompromising blue sky, mountains never too distant, a shift in weather never too far away.

When we came here from Portugal, it seemed the right decision to be near so much opportunity and to be safe away from the grasping hands of the Inquisition. In these lowlands, the church does not hold the same power in the same way as it did in Sepharad. Perhaps because we were never rooted here. Then again, how can one root where the land is always being swallowed by water? And what appeared to me, first as kindness, now seems to be indifference.

I still have not mastered the local tongue and usually converse in French to the Christians. At home, between us, we speak Castilian and at times Arabic, both of which flow so much more easily, like song and breath. I find it hard to make these guttural sounds but have learned enough at least to help in my uncle's export and import trade. This is a place of ships, of leavings and comings, and it makes me want to leave all the more.

But today, I will go and fetch just the right ingredients to make the bunuelos we always loved. I will top them with honey and serve them at the hour of the merienda. We still keep our customs here within our home. This one I will keep as well.

I have written to Diego Colon who was friends of a sort with Papa at the court. I have written to ask him what more he knows of the lands his father has found. I know Louis de Torres went with him on his journey and I believe he stayed behind there when Colon returned. I wonder who else is there with him. I wonder if there could ever be another home for me on those islands, in a place I cannot quite imagine, under skies that would not be the blue of home nor the gray of these Netherlands.

I have heard through other correspondences that the lands there are lush with fish jumping from the waters, and foods growing from the earth that barely need tending. And then I think of never seeing my Sarah again, not having the comfort of her and Isaac, not knowing the nephews and nieces I will have not so long from now. I think and I don't know if I can bear to leave them anymore than I can bear to stay.

I lift the teapot my aunt and uncle brought with them. They keep it on the mantel. It is heavy to lift and heavy to hold, because of all it contains. It is a called a Hidden Synagogue because it holds secret pieces. Remove the top and there is a hidden dreidel, remove the next layer and there is a spice holder. The next layer holds a place for the eternal flame, as well as an inscription in Hebrew that reads, "The light of G-d is man's soul." But there are more secrets still, a complete Megillah, the Book of Esther, that we read at the festival of Purim. The main body is designed to hold an Etrog, the yellow citron for the Sukkot, and it is curved to fit a menorah for Chanukah. And inside, candlesticks for Shabbos, and under the candlesticks a Seder plate for Passover. It is magic in a way. It makes me laugh to think we carry the year's festivals disguised as a teapot.

I wish it would stop raining. I wish, I wish. I will go and do the baking. I will sink my hands deep in the flour and mix in the milk and eggs and I will make Sarah smile. At least I can do that. It is nothing I have to wish for, it is something I can do. I only know I want to leave this dark city of water, these low skies and flat lands. Amsterdam offered a place to shelter when there was no other, but it has never felt like home. It is a small cloaked room in which we can hide but I do not want to feel like I am hiding forever.

Then, I heard his voice. At first, I thought it must be just my imagination. I paused as if to look into a shop I was passing, but there it was again.

"Chava, Chava."

I turned and it was Daniel. I stood still, holding the basket of goods I was carrying, looking at them. But what I saw was myself dropping the basket and running toward him, pressing into him, seeking out the assurance that indeed we were both here, in this moment, this place. Though I did not move. I stood still and waited.

"Please, Chava, I have been looking for you. I arrived from Venice early this morning. Please can we talk?"

His eyes seemed even darker than I remembered, caverns. He had grown taller, and fuller, stronger. He was no longer a boy. But he was still the one that had left me. I stood silently. I looked at him and then looked down.

"How much do you know of my life these past years?"

"I have been in correspondence with Isaac. I know the trajectory of your travels. I know Isaac and Sarah married. I know you have not. But beyond his own personal affairs, Isaac would not answer my questions about you except to say that you were well."

"I am glad someone is loyal, at least."

"Chava, is there someone else?"

I looked at him then, really looked, and saw the anguish in him. It squelched my desire to say yes there was someone else, to lash out at him as his leaving had lashed and lacerated me. But really there was no one else. There were men who had approached, but they left me indifferent. I preferred the company of my books, my work, my sister and brother-in-law.

"Please Chava, can we talk?" He asked again, his hand moving as if to reach for mine. I watched him draw it back, draw himself in.

I could not have hesitated for more than half a minute, but it felt a very long time as I considered whether to let him back into my life again or not. In that breath of a moment I felt the wood of the old puzzle box in my hands. The box where I had kept the words he had given back to me. I recalled the brush of his hand against my young cheek as we stood in the garden.

I knew he was still as much home to me as Spain. "Yes. Come to the house in an hour. You know where we live, I presume." Inside I was bursting. An old song fluttered through me as if I were still young girl and there was a whisper just under my tongue, "My Daniel." But on the outside I was stern, even cold.

He bowed to me and said, "I will see you in an hour then."

It took all my strength not to run through the streets like a child. I admit I did walk quickly and when I opened the door, I shouted Sarah's name.

"He found you?" She asked, taking the basket from my hands.

"How did you know?"

"He came here looking for you. You know that he has been writing."

"Isaac mentioned it." I said. But I did not realize how often, or how earnestly he had been sending letters.

"He has shed his conversion. You know he has cut himself off from his family?"

"No," was all I could muster.

"He went to Portugal after we left and helped others leave."

"But then why did he take so long to come here?"

"I think he was afraid to see you, Chava. I think he needed to make himself whole again."

" I know we were barely more than children, but he should have stood by me. He never should have…"

"Chava, what would you have done if Mama and Papa demanded that you to convert and said it was the only way to save their lives and moved us all away?

"I would have asked him to come."

"Yes, and what did he do?"

"But he knew I would not. He knew that."

"It seems, sister, you will have another chance to decide what to do again."

"What do you mean?"

"I only know Daniel has come here to speak with you. Go take a few minutes to compose yourself. He will be here soon."

Over the next weeks Daniel and I spent more hours together every day. There was no denying that the love we had as children had not gone away. No wonder I had not cared about other men, not even the best of them made me feel as I found myself with Daniel. Both at home and as if I were on an adventure at once. By the end of the year, Daniel and I were married.

Here we were, as it had all been planned so long ago, although Sarah and Isaac had wed first, and our parents were not with us. Still, Amsterdam did not feel like home. It was kind enough to us after our travails, it offered a quiet, a stability, Uncle and Aunt were now established here. We all lived in a house that was commodious, but it was too dark and dreary for me.

Uncle and Aunt would stay here. Sarah and Isaac were not yet sure. They were looking east, perhaps to Salonica, where it had been made plain that we would be welcome. We talked of settling there. What it would be like to live in a bustling city, a mix of languages and people coming and going. And yet we did not leave. Soon it would be almost five years since we had left Spain behind. We lit the Yahrzeit candles for Isaac's parents and for ours. Sarah had one child with another on the way. We still spoke of going east, even as far as Jerusalem, but we did not want to leave our aunt and uncle. We kept what family we had left as close as we could.

Colon had completed two voyages; the second taking settlers to the islands. There was talk of a third voyage. And then Daniel had another idea. He wanted to go west. He reminded me of the dreams I had as a child when I first heard of Colon's plans to sail west to find the east. I wrote again to Diego Colon as I had not yet heard back from him. I knew that he had cousins that were Conversos. We knew of others who had stayed behind on the islands and let fall the pretense of being new Christians, far from the eyes and ears of the Inquisition. While the voyage would have to be taken in the guise of being a new Christian, once we were there we would not need to pretend.

There was a small island, beyond Hispaniola, where a group had settled and was beginning a new community. I began to see again the brightly colored birds of Granada. I imagined the sea toques instead of this dull, lowland brown. I imagined a place where the wind did not bite into a chill but caressed away the heat. And I imagined my life with Daniel, the one I had shut away in my puzzle box and not opened since we had left Toledo. And yet still I carried it with me from place to place. Daniel and I would walk along the canals and imagine what that other world might look like. In the summer light we caught sight of storks circling their nests. We learned their name in Dutch meant the treasure bringers. Well, Amsterdam had brought Daniel back to me.

We spent another cold winter in Amsterdam. My cousin lived with his aunt and uncle in the house next door to Sarah and Isaac, Daniel and me. We had Shabbat dinner together every week. My aunt and uncle had become grandparents, and Isaac and Sarah would soon have their second child. Daniel and I kept talking about the lands that lay beyond the sea and then, as if overnight, there were dates and routes and a place on a ship.

Colon would set forth the following year on his third voyage. We would meet his ships on Gomera and go to the new world. My niece, Estrella, was born and I stayed to help Sarah in the first months of being a mother of two, and then we left for the Canary Islands, west and then further west still to make a new home. We carried with us only a few possessions, some books, the manuscript mother had entrusted to me, a set of candlesticks, that little turquoise elephant amongst them and the secret teapot gifted to us by my aunt and uncle.

And then the things that took no room, the memories of our childhoods, the blessings of our parents, the memorized words of poems and prayer.

Chapter Fourteen

The New World

CHAVA

I still have that handkerchief, the one I carried down the terraces in Mieza, and it still holds the scent of spring in Spain. I have kept these few precious things in my trunk, the journal, the quill, the handkerchief, and even a nub of the candle we lit for that last time in Spain. For so many years I tried to conjure the image of my mother, and then for so many more I didn't try at all. It was too painful, and I was sure that she had died. But lately I can see her face again. Her thick dark hair that was going silver around the temples, her deep blue eyes and the worry lines around her mouth. When Sarah and I were little she would take us walking out past the city. We would stop by the river and toss stones and she would laugh and say, "Toss another worry away my girls! There is no use in holding on to them."

The year I turned 50, I decided it was time to fill the very last page left in the journal my mother gave me so many years ago. At first, I was not sure what I would write.

I kept thinking of the conversations Sarah and I had with mother in the days before I left, my promise to write her. Her request that I commit our story to these pages. I imagine somehow, she will come to know the thoughts I share here, one last letter as I remember her.

Querida Mama

I see you still by the ledge of the window at the cross of the stairs before they make their way from the landing up to the second floor. I see you leaning there looking at your household. You never let your status as mistress of the house keep you from knowing the work of the house.

You taught me that each task imbued with attention becomes work that is filled with love. You are leaning forward into the light of the open window and the scent of roses from our garden rises up to meet you. You look pleased, the lines of your face gone so your skin is as soft as the petals of the flowers you take such pleasure in.

Mama I am older now than you were then. I rest my arms on the wooden ledge of the rough window here in this new world where we have come to replant our family's tree. Here on this island where there is always the sound of the waters that could carry me home. I have replanted myself, and my youngest daughter will wed tomorrow.

I never saw you become an old woman. I never saw you bend toward the ground, walking hesitantly, straining to see. I never saw you reach for something and then give up. I never saw you give up. When we left your hair was just beginning to be stranded with gray and white. When we left you waved goodbye to us as if we were off for a walk and a picnic in the bend of the river. How your heart must have been breaking, Mama. Mine was.

But now, having a daughter, now I know that it did not just feel like it was tearing, it was tearing. I hope you found sustenance. I hope you found some joy in your days, that accomplishing what you needed to do gave you some peace.

I have taken your strength and transplanted it here. After the crossing I was weak and tired and disillusioned. I thought we should have stayed in Amsterdam. I thought we should have gone east to Poland or Turkey instead of the long voyage to this small, fragile island. I thought at least we should have remained on the same mass of land that had always held our family.

But somehow west seemed the right direction Mama, away from what we knew to something new and unknown. We have made a life here, it is different of course. There are not so many of us, and we have learned to work together, which is not to say we don't discuss and argue and debate. I studied the words you sent with me and I have shared them. I think of you and father every day. I miss Sarah so, but I know she is happy with Isaac and their growing family. I am grateful I learned from you that questioning was not just for the words in the texts we loved, but for the everyday as well.

We have kept our customs but shaped them to this land, where our homes let in the tropical light and air, where we are all gardeners, men and women working together. We share the island with people whose history we do not know or understand, just as they do not understand ours. I can only hope we will learn to live here together in peace.

For now, I will not recount the work of it, but I want to tell you that tomorrow we will dance in this place. We will dance.

Shana Ritter is originally from New York but has lived out in the country near Bloomington, Indiana for a very long time. She previously lived in Spain and returns to visit often.

In the Time of Leaving is her first novel. It began with a poem that came unbidden when walking late at night in the old Barrio Judeo in Toledo, Spain.

Her poetry and short stories have appeared in Lilith, Fifth Wednesday, Georgetown Review and others. Her chapbook, Stairs of Separation was published by Finishing Line Press.

Shana has been noiminat4ed for a Pushcart, and been awarded the Indiana Individual Artist Grant multiple times.

Made in the USA
Lexington, KY
20 May 2019